P9-ECJ-294

Diane felt foolish,
Compliments!

Was it that simple? Was she reading too much into the things he'd said? "I'm sorry, I . . . perhaps I should just say thank you, kind sir." She added with a smile, still feeling foolish, "It's just that—I thought you were flirting with me."

Dominik looked delighted, and more amused than ever. "But I was flirting with you. So what—is that so terrible?"

It made things worse. He was absolutely right, of course. Exasperated, she wondered about his effect on her, why she was so tongue-tied.

Before she could think what to say, Dominik crossed over, picked up her hand and pressed his lips to the back of it. "It's very nice to know you, Diane West," he said, "and I look forward to discovering more."

Claudia Jameson lives in Berkshire, England, with her husband and family. She is an extremely popular author in both the Harlequin Presents and Harlequin Romance series. And no wonder! Her lively dialogue and ingenious plots—with the occasional dash of suspense—make her a favorite with romance readers everywhere.

Books by Claudia Jameson

HARLEQUIN ROMANCE

HARLEQUIN PRESENTS

Don't miss any of our special offers. Write to us at the following address for information on our newest releases.

Harlequin Reader Service
901 Fuhrmann Blvd., P.O. Box 1397, Buffalo, NY 14240
Canadian address: P.O. Box 603,
Fort Erie, Ont. L2A 5X3

That Certain Yearning

Claudia Jameson

Harlequin Books

TORONTO • NEW YORK • LONDON
AMSTERDAM • PARIS • SYDNEY • HAMBURG
STOCKHOLM • ATHENS • TOKYO • MILAN

Original hardcover edition published in 1989
by Mills & Boon Limited

ISBN 0-373-03046-0

Harlequin Romance first edition April 1990

Copyright © 1989 by Claudia Jameson.
All rights reserved. Except for use in any review, the reproduction or utilization
of this work in whole or in part in any form by any electronic, mechanical or
other means, now known or hereafter invented, including xerography,
photocopying and recording, or in any information storage or retrieval system,
is forbidden without the permission of the publisher, Harlequin Enterprises
Limited, 225 Duncan Mill Road, Don Mills, Ontario, Canada M3B 3K9.

All the characters in this book have no existence outside the imagination of
the author and have no relation whatsoever to anyone bearing the same name
or names. They are not even distantly inspired by any individual known or
unknown to the author, and all incidents are pure invention.

® are Trademarks registered in the United States Patent and Trademark Office
and in other countries.

Printed in U.S.A.

CHAPTER ONE

EDEN COTTAGE looked very pleasant from the outside, covered as it was with clinging ivy, its front garden a profusion of roses in full bloom. It was nine-thirty in the evening by the time Diane West pulled up outside it, but there was still plenty of light and she was impressed by what she could see. There was no telephone in the property, but she was very glad of that; she had thought it an advantage when she'd committed herself to renting the place for two weeks. Not that she would be incommunicado here. She had left the address of the cottage with three different people just in case of a dire emergency—and she had warned them all not to disturb her for anything less.

Actually, she probably wouldn't stay the full two weeks. Ten days should be enough, enough time in which to think and sort herself out. By then she should have come to terms with her father having remarried . . . no, it wasn't his remarrying, it was *whom* he had married that bothered her so much. Whom and why.

Escaping to the Bournemouth area had been a sudden decision, and she had been very lucky indeed to be able to rent anything at all at such short notice, given that it would be August in a couple of days, the height of the holiday season in England. A last-minute cancellation had made it possible, according to the woman in the office at the letting company, a Mrs Archer.

'It is short notice,' she'd said to Diane, 'but as it happens we can oblige because I've just had a cancellation on a booking for Eden Cottage, which is a few miles outside Boscombe. It's one of our prettier properties, terraced, with a small front garden and a big, fenced garden at the back. It's fully equipped and nicely furnished but there's no telephone. Still, I can offer you a reduced rate, since it's just for yourself . . .'

The only hitch had been Diane's inability to collect the key before the office, which was in Christchurch, closed at noon on the Saturday. 'I just can't make it,' she had explained to Mrs Archer. 'My father's getting married on Saturday and there's no way I can get to Dorset until the evening. I'll put my cheque in the post straight away, of course, but I can't guarantee that getting to you by Saturday, either.'

There had been a momentary silence during which Diane closed her eyes, expecting to be disappointed, expecting to be told that in the circumstances she could not have Eden Cottage until the Monday.

Instead she was told there was no problem. 'Not to worry, Miss West. With a little luck I'll be able to leave the key next door for you, next door to the cottage, I mean. But I'll have to make a telephone call first, to make sure it'll be all right. May I ring you back? I'm sure I can sort this out in ten minutes or so . . .'

It had all been very simple in the end, had all worked out beautifully—for here she was, with two suitcases and a big carton of groceries in the back of her estate car. She almost smiled, almost but not quite; she had spent the entire day having to smile at the wedding and the reception, false smiles, continual efforts to hide her anxiety for her father and his future, and, for his sake, efforts to camouflage the resentment she felt towards his new wife.

She got out of her car and determinedly pushed thoughts

of Annabel aside. Thinking about her now was pointless; Annabel was on honeymoon with her new husband and, if she were giving any thought at all to Diane right now, it would no doubt be with triumphant amusement. The woman had got what she wanted; she had won.

Force of habit made Diane lock her car; she didn't stop to think about it but instead was distracted by the stiffness of her limbs, by the pleasant prospect of a long, hot bath. The drive from Maidstone had been nothing to her, as a manufacturers' agent she was used to driving many miles in the course of a day, but the tension of this particular day had got to her and she was tired both physically and mentally.

The cottage to the right of hers was Rose Cottage, aptly named because it, too, had masses of roses in its garden. She rang the doorbell and waited, trying to remember the name of the man from whom she was to collect her key. When the door swung open quite suddenly she was bombarded with several impressions, information it took her several moments to assimilate.

Above the soft strains of Beethoven emanating from behind the man facing her there came the shrill cry of a child, a girl-child by the sound of it. Then there was the startling appearance of a Great Dane, barking its head off. Added to this there was the man's obvious agitation, the swift, black look he threw at Diane before commanding the dog to silence and to sit. He turned his head towards the staircase, looking up. 'Come in for a moment.' The words were snapped out to Diane as he retreated, moving rapidly up the stairs, leaving her feeling bewildered and doubtful on the doorstep, eyeing the dog—who was eyeing her. Had she come to the right cottage? What was going on? The cry from above had become heaving sobs now, a heart-rending noise which made Diane herself want to dash upstairs. Mr Chandler's child was having a nightmare, no doubt.

It was a girl, wasn't it? And his name was Chandler? Diane hesitantly stepped inside, expecting to see someone else—Mrs Chandler, for example—but there was no one, nothing except the dog and the music and the glow of a standard lamp in the corner of the living-room beyond the hallway. She hovered between the two, leaning wearily on the doorframe while keeping her eyes on both the dog and the stairs. Though the sounds of distress from up there had quickly been silenced, it was several minutes before the man came down again and, when he did, the very first impression Diane had had became fixed and sure in her mind. It was, simply, that he was very preoccupied, worried about something. His eyes were on her now, but he was not seeing her. Abruptly he said he supposed she was Miss West, that she had come for the key to Eden Cottage.

That the man was looking through her did not bother Diane; she was looking at him, and she was doing so with a sense of shock. He was beautiful—there was no other word for it. Like her, he had hair as black as coal, as straight and as thick as her own, brushed carelessly straight back from his forehead. Unlike her, he had brown eyes, dark and unfathomable, warm and yet distant. Of themselves they were beautiful, but in that particular face, with that particular bone-structure, so masculine and aristocratic too, they were in the most perfect setting. Without breaking from that unseeing look of his, her own eyes absorbed the total picture of him. Blue denim jeans and shirt, the latter well-worn and faded, rolled up at the sleeves and open at the neck, enough to expose the short, springy curls of hair there. Tall and broad, but slim without being rangy, he seemed so fit and vital. Energy seemed to pour out of him even as he stood motionless, like an aura which was at once both alluring and dangerous . . .

The sudden clenching of his jaw-bone, the silent click of a muscle movement as he snapped out words she didn't hear, was enough to make her feel like an idiot. She had been staring at him, rudely, with far too much interest. It was not at all like her, either; it was quite out of character for her to respond to a male, to any male, like that.

'I—yes. I am Diane West.' She made herself smile. It would be her last manufactured smile of the day, and she hoped it was appropriate. What had he just said? 'And you're Mr Chandler, I take it?'

'Channing.' Moving closer to her, he repeated the name firmly, offering his hand. Diane couldn't be sure whether he'd spoken with a hint of a smile this time. In spite of herself, her eyes were drawn to his mouth as she wondered whether its corners had just twitched slightly. '*Channing*. Dominik Channing.'

'How do you do?' She took the proffered hand and knew without a doubt now what was happening. Whether Mr Channing felt it too, she had no idea, but she herself was experiencing an attraction to this total stranger. It had been there the second she had set eyes on him, before this hand-to-hand contact, and it shook her now she was forced to acknowledge it. A little too abruptly she pulled her hand away, her eyes flicking guiltily in the direction of the stairs, then towards the kitchen. She was expecting Mrs Channing to appear at any second. 'I'm—I'll take the key then, Mr Channing. I'm rather tired and——'

He had already moved away, clearly uninterested and with no desire to detain her. Seconds later he was back with a key in his open palm and, knowing the stupidity of her action, Diane made every effort not to make physical con-

tact as she took it from him. She failed, of course, and spoke
brusquely to hide a feeling of confusion, of irritation with
herself. 'Isn't there a back door key?'

'It's in the lock.'

'Oh. Well, I'll say goodnight, then.'

'Goodnight, Miss West.' He swung the front door open
and closed it quickly the moment she was out of the way, so
quickly that it irked her. No one wanted peace and quiet
more than she did right now, but did he have to be that
obvious in his resentment of her intrusion?

She turned to glance at the lighted bedroom window,
wondering. Maybe his wife was upstairs, with the
daughter? Perhaps it had been more serious than a
nightmare, maybe the child was ill and Dominik Channing
had been anxious to go back upstairs?

Within fifteen minutes she had forgotten the encounter
with her neighbour, her box of groceries was on the
draining board, waiting to be unpacked, and her suitcases
were in one of the two bedrooms. She had opted to sleep in
the double room rather than the twin, just for the pleasure
of being in a double bed again, of having space again. For
the past week she had been sleeping in a foldaway bed in the
box-room at home in her father's bungalow, because her
own bedroom had been taken over by Annabel and her
eight-year-old son, Bobby. Not that Bobby was any trouble;
far from it, he was a delight to have around—which was
much more than could be said for his mother.

Annabel had been so casual, so cold-blooded about her
arrangements! Three days ago she had driven Bobby to
Scotland in order to deposit him with his father. That
Bobby had wanted to be at his mother's wedding to Frank
West had made no difference to her, she had not allowed it.
She had packed him off to the man she had divorced six

years earlier, the man who hadn't wanted to know his own son—or so her story went. If it were true, then why was he willing to have Bobby for two weeks now, while Annabel went on her honeymoon?

'Damn!' Resignedly, Diane turned off the taps in the bathroom. There was no hot water. She had let it run and run and—there simply was no hot water. There was central heating in the cottage, but it was off at this time of year, obviously. So what was she supposed to do? Surely there was a separate control for the water, even if one didn't have the heating on? There wasn't. She found the thermostat in the hall but there was no separate control for hot water. In that case she would have to switch on the immersion heater and wait. She was hot and sticky and there was no way she was going to bed without washing.

'Fine,' she said aloud, upstairs again, knowing a mounting sense of frustration, 'but where's the switch?' The airing cupboard was large, well-stocked with linens and towels—but there was no switch for the immersion heater.

Ten minutes later she knew there was nothing for it but to seek help. The idea did not appeal to her, but it was tough luck. It was, after all, only just turned ten, so her neighbours wouldn't be in bed yet, any of them. If there was a sign of life in the house on the other side of Eden Cottage, she would ask them for a clue. Chances were that the system was the same in all the cottages; there were four in the row and the woman in the letting office had said the company owned them all.

There was no answer from either of the other two, so Diane had no choice but to ring the bell of Rose Cottage, bracing herself, rehearsing what she would say.

The door was answered by Dominik Channing and she was word-perfect . . . as far as she got. 'I'm sorry to disturb you again, Mr Channing, but——'

'That makes two of us.'

She stared at him in dismay, taken aback by his rudeness. Strains of Mozart were reaching her now—not that she registered what she was hearing, for she couldn't get over this man's attitude. She could see no warmth in the beautiful eyes now, only the distance in them. 'I won't come in,' she said at length, with as much sarcasm as she could muster. 'If you'll just tell me where I might find the switch for the immersion heater, I'll go.'

There was a pause, there was a hint of a smile, or so it seemed, and then, 'And will you never darken my doorstep again?'

'What?' Diane was staring at him again. Was he joking? Had he smiled, or nearly smiled, or was she imagining it?

'I believe you heard me, Miss West.'

Yes, she had, and it made no difference that he really was smiling now, a smile that actually made her heart skip a beat. Angry with herself as much as with him, she decided it was high time he understood what she was about. 'Indeed did, and this is no social call, believe me. It's quite obvious that you and your family keep yourselves to yourselves, but don't worry, that's precisely what *I* intend to do. I've rented this cottage for some peace and quiet, as you have, no doubt, so if you'll just tell me——'

'It's in the airing cupboard.' His black brows had risen, as if her outburst had served only to amuse him.

'But it isn't. I've looked.'

'Then look again, Miss West.'

Diane stuck her hands on her hips. This was not proving to be the evening she had anticipated, away from it all, with no aggravation for a change. 'Mr Channing, I am neither blind nor stupid. I've——'

'It is in the airing cupboard, behind what appears to be panelling, to the right. It's one of those cupboards which opens not with a handle but by pushing. Do that and it will click open, hey presto! Try it and see.'

She nodded in silence, closing her eyes and feeling idiotic again. Why hadn't she thought of that? Why hadn't it occurred to her that those were cupboards along the wall? With muttered thanks she retreated, ignoring the amusement in his voice as he called after her.

'Will there be anything else, Miss West? Some milk or a cup of sugar, perhaps?'

She was trembling with frustration when she got indoors. The man's attitude was hateful. Did he think she'd gone back to see him just for the fun of it? Was he one of those men who adored their own attractiveness, who took pleasure in the effect he had on women, whether he was married or not? It was a horrid thought, she could only hope she had given no clue at all about the physical attraction she'd reluctantly felt earlier. It was gone now, anyhow. It had just been a silly chemical response—or something. In any case, he was the perfect example of beauty being only skin-deep; she could never be really attracted to a man like that, a boorish clever-clogs who didn't have the basic good manners of—of a cat!

It started raining around midnight. She had been in bed for an hour and was still unable to sleep, not that there was one thing in particular on her mind. Her father was, after all, fifty-three years old and in command of all his faculties. It was just that he was so blind as far as Annabel was concerned . . . but the prospect of moving out of the bungalow wasn't so awful. She was perfectly grown up herself, and more than capable of looking out for herself. But what was the point in this? She was going over old ground, old thoughts, yet again. It had to stop. Annabel was now Mrs Frank West, and that was that. Diane had a step-mother, at least technically, whether she wanted one or not, a stepmother who was just nine years her senior. Oh, Annabel had said all the right things, of course, both privately to Diane and in front of Frank. That was all part of her cunning. She had appeared sincere when she had urged Diane not to go ahead with the purchase of a flat.

'But, Diane, this is your home!' she'd said, as if she were at a loss. 'Why should you move out?'

'Because there isn't room for all of us, Annabel.' As if she'd needed telling. 'There are only three bedrooms.'

'But that's all we need, three bedrooms is exactly what we need.'

Except that there would be nowhere for Diane to hang her samples. Except that you couldn't swing a cat in the box-room, except that Bobby was a growing boy who needed space, somewhere to play, except that there was only one lavatory, one bathroom in the bungalow. Except—but it wasn't that, any of it, not really. Diane was moving out because she could not stand to watch Annabel's manipulation of her father, because she hated to see how besotted he was with the woman, because he was acting like an old fool.

It was still raining at one-thirty in the morning. That was the last time Diane glanced at the clock before finally drifting to sleep. She remembered seeing the time, remembered thinking it didn't matter if she slept late, it was Sunday tomorrow, and in any case she was on a holiday of sorts.

When she opened her eyes the next day, she remembered also that she had hoped for better weather—and this was one hope fulfilled. The bedroom curtains were honey-coloured and the sun was streaming through them. She flung them open and looked down into the garden at the back, a generous rectangle of grass, completely private, enclosed by a high, latticed fence on all sides.

Her plans for the day were made instantly: all she would do was—nothing! What bliss that would be, to lie in the garden and do nothing. She had not slept late, after all, and by ten o'clock she was washed and dressed in a new bikini of the palest pink. Quite deliberately she had chosen a bikini which was almost flesh-coloured—to make less of a contrast against the paleness of her skin. It had been a long time since she had lain in the sun.

Her reflection in the bathroom mirror pleased her: very clear, very green eyes looked back at her, trimmed as they were with thick black lashes. Her eyes were her best feature and, in her opinion, it was much to be thankful for because the rest of her face was nothing to write home about. She would have preferred fuller lips and a nose which wasn't quite as long, for example. Still, people told her she was attractive, and her figure was undeniably good. It was nice to be tall and slim, a definite advantage to be able to model, when necessary, the clothes she sold.

Ten minutes later, having brushed her hair into a ponytail, she was lying outside on a white bath-towel, draped on a sun-lounger she had found in a cupboard under the stairs. She had applied a generous coating of sun-cream and had just settled down to the serious business of sun-bathing, eyes closed, when she heard a voice.

'I'm thirsty.'

When the message was repeated, Diane opened her eyes, realising that it was she who was being spoken to. She saw the child from Rose Cottage through the gaps in the lattice-work of the fence, standing close to it, peering as best she

could at Diane, who smiled. So this was Dominik
Channing's daughter, a girl of ten or eleven. Amazing that
her hair was so blonde when her father's was so black.

'Well, if you're thirsty, why don't you go indoors and get
a drink?'

There was laughter. 'Not *thirsty*! I didn't say I was
thirsty, I said I was *Kirsty*. That's my name, Kirsty.'

'Oh!' Diane was laughing, too. 'Sorry about that! So,
Kirsty, how are you today?'

'I'm fine, thank you. I'm always well. How are you? Who
are you? I mean, what's your name?'

'I'm Diane West and I'm very well too, thank you.'

'Are you on holiday?'

'Yes.'

'We're supposed to be on holiday but it isn't—I can't see
you properly. Can I come through? Is the gate locked on
your side?'

The gate was actually a door in the fence, further down
the garden by the house. Diane hadn't even registered its
existence. She got up to investigate, smiling her surprise on
seeing the girl's face properly. She was so lovely! She might
not have inherited her father's hair colour but she had
certainly inherited his good looks.

A moment later Diane realised her mistake, when she
climbed back on to the lounger and Kirsty plonked herself
down on the grass—white shorts and all. 'I'm waiting to go
to the beach, Diane, but Uncle Nik's talking to his solicitor
on the telephone and that takes *ages*. He's always on the
phone and he talks to his office every morning during week-
days, so this isn't really a holiday, not a proper one. Not for
him, anyhow.'

So Dominik Channing was her uncle. In that case, 'Well,
where's your aunt? Couldn't she take you to the beach?'

This was met with puzzlement. 'My aunt? What do you—oh, you mean Uncle Nik's wife? He hasn't got one. He nearly had one, last year, but he decided he didn't like her in the end. I didn't like her, either,' she added. Then, as if it were relevant, 'She was twenty-nine. How old are you?'

'Twenty-four.' Diane grinned. 'Twenty-four and three months, to be precise.'

'Well, I'm nearly eleven. It's my birthday next week, on Wednesday. I don't mean this coming Wednesday, but the one after.'

Kirsty, whose surname, Diane learned, was Nolan, was not only a chatterbox but also very young for her years. While she was obviously happy to impart information about her Uncle Nik, however, the child said nothing about her parents and, for some reason she could not fathom, Diane resisted the temptation to ask about them.

'I wish Uncle Nik would hurry up. He even has a telephone in his car, you know.'

Diane thought about that; she had seen no other vehicle outside the cottages, only her own. 'Where is his car?'

The girl gestured towards some garages beyond the garden. 'In the garage over there. Those garages belong to these cottages, didn't you know?'

'No, I . . .' The woman in the letting office had not mentioned there was a garage. 'Well, I'm happy to leave my car at the front, anyway.'

'And where's your husband, Diane? Oh, you're not wearing a wedding ring, are you? You're not even engaged.'

Diane laughed at that. 'No, not even.'

'But you're not on holiday by yourself, are you? Haven't you got——?'

The child was cut off in mid-sentence. Dominik Channing, and the Great Dane, appeared in the garden next door. 'Kirsty? Where the devil are you?'

She shot to her feet and started waving. 'I'm here! Next door. I'm talking to Diane.'

The reply to that was stern and straight to the point. 'Miss West to you. Now move yourself. Miss West is here for peace and quiet and she does not want——' He didn't finish saying what Diane did not want, not immediately. He had walked up to the fence and, at his height of six feet two or thereabouts, was easily tall enough to see over it.

It required an effort of will for Diane not to move, not to change position, not to be obvious in her self-consciousness. It wasn't easy, because Dominik Channing allowed himself a blatant inspection of her, of every inch of her near-nakedness. He didn't take long to do so but he was thorough, his eyes scanning every curve of her long, slender body. That all his concentration was then shifted to his niece, and the fact that it stayed there did nothing to lessen the rush of irritation his flagrant scrutiny had provoked in Diane.

The irritation was added to when he went on to tell Kirsty that in no circumstances was she to disturb her. The child was not a disturbance to Diane; far from it, she liked children. They were always so easy to get on with . . . which was more than could be said for a lot of adults. 'I assure you, Mr Channing,' she put in quickly, 'Kirsty is not disturbing me.'

'Which is very polite of you,' he countered, not looking at her at all now, 'but it's not the case. Kirsty—come.'

The girl shot a confused look at Diane, as if to say she had had quite a different impression. With a hasty apology, something else which added to Diane's irritation with her neighbour, she went back to the garden of Rose Cottage and was ushered, together with the big dog, through the kitchen door.

CHAPTER TWO

DIANE saw nothing else of her neighbours for the rest of the day, and it was by sheer coincidence that she saw them that evening, in a local restaurant she had noticed on the way down to the cottage. Her day of laziness had made her really idle, so much so that she decided to eat out instead of cooking, to have an early dinner in what proved to be a very cosy family restaurant about a mile away.

She walked there because it was such a fine night, and it was not until she was seated at a small table for two that she had any idea Dominik Channing was in the restaurant. It was the sudden appearance of Kirsty that alerted her.

'Uncle Nik's in the Gents',' the young voice said, coming from immediately behind Diane. 'And we're sitting over there—you didn't see me, did you?'

'Hello, Kirsty. No, I didn't, I'm afraid.'

There was a shrug, a look of uncertainty. 'Is it true, Diane? Don't you want me to talk to you? Have I got to leave you alone like Uncle Nik said?'

Diane smiled warmly, hoping to cover her feeling of awkwardness. 'No, actually it isn't. You see—er—there's been a misunderstanding. I did tell your uncle that I wanted peace and quiet, but that didn't apply to you, Kirsty. I like chatting to you.'

The child's smile was triumphant, knowing. 'That's what I thought! I *told* him you were friendly, but he didn't believe me. I told him——'

'Kirsty—your uncle, he's back and he's looking for you.

19

You'd better go over to him.' Dominik Channing was back at the table on the other side of the restaurant. He spotted his niece and frowned. 'Go on, poppet.'

'Oh. Yes, OK. Anyway, we've had our dinner so we're going back to the cottage now—but I'll see you in the morning, Diane. I can see you when Uncle Nik's on the phone to his office.'

When she had nothing better to do, Diane thought, grinning. What was she doing on holiday with her uncle, anyway, one in which Dominik Channing could not wholly participate? Why was he talking to his office every day if he was on holiday? Where were Kirsty's parents? Abroad, perhaps? Or maybe they were ill and he was caretaking for a while? But why bother renting a cottage for the purpose when he surely had a home of his own somewhere?

She turned to look out of the window, suddenly realising that the mystery of her neighbours had distracted her from her own preoccupations. Well, that was a good thing, because in fact there was little she could do about her own life now except wait. She was waiting for completion on the flat she'd bought in Maidstone, far enough but not too far away from her father's bungalow. In truth, had she wanted only peace and quiet she could just as easily have stayed at the bungalow while her father and Annabel were on honeymoon. But there would have been distractions of another kind there, like the way Annabel had already stamped her personality all over the place. No, it had been right to come away, to have a change of scenery until she could move into her own place. Maybe she would go to the beach tomorrow, weather permitting.

The weather did permit. She woke to find a day just as sunny as the previous one, and by nine-thirty she was break-fasted, dressed and having a cup of coffee in the kitchen when Kirsty turned up.

'Hello, Diane. Is it all right if Penny comes in?'

The Great Dane was looking at Diane with doleful eyes, her tail wagging frantically. They had obviously got sufficiently acquainted not to merit any more barking—at least for the moment.

'Of course she can.'

'Do you like dogs?' Kirsty, who was not the most graceful of girls, sat herself at the kitchen table cowboy fashion, her legs straddled either side of the chair.

'Yes, though I've never owned one. You look as if you're all set for the beach again, Kirsty. Is that a swimsuit under those shorts?'

'Yes.' The child's blue eyes were lit with anticipation. 'We're spending the whole day there, if it stays sunny. As soon as Uncle Nik gets off the phone,' she added, looking heavenward. When she saw Diane's reaction was one of laughter, she did it again. 'There's no telephone in here, I know. That's why we took the cottage next door. Mrs Archer at the office had messed up the bookings again, you know. She's always doing it. Still, it was just as well, otherwise we'd have had to stay in a hotel and that's boring.'

Diane was lost. 'Mrs Archer? The lady who does the lettings? But how do you know all this? I mean, how do you know she'd messed up the bookings? She told me she'd had a last-minute cancellation.'

'Not true.' Kirsty shook her head vehemently. 'I know all about it because Uncle Nik owns these cottages. He's got property all over the place, you know.'

'I—oh! No, I didn't know.'

'Mm. Well, what I should say is that he's the company who owns them,' she added gravely. 'It means the same thing, really. Do you know what people call him? Dynamic.

That means he's very busy, that's why he's always seeing to business in the mornings. He's a businessman.'

Bemused by this new information, Diane had to suppress her laughter this time. 'Yes, well, businessmen do tend to do business, Kirsty.'

The remark was lost on her, she was still looking intensely serious. 'Anyway, I told him—about us, I mean.'

Diane wondered what was coming next, she got up to put the kettle on for more coffee. 'About us?'

'Mm. I explained to him about that misunderstanding you told me of last night, in the restaurant. I told him you like talking to me, that it's *him* you don't want to talk to.'

The older girl didn't know whether to laugh or to groan. Well, that had certainly fixed things! If she had thought Dominik Channing stand-offish, unfriendly, he would no doubt be convinced that *she* was positively antisocial, at least as far as adults were concerned. Perhaps it was just as well; the man fancied himself and was too cocky for her liking. In any case, she really couldn't care less whether she ever spoke to him again.

But she did speak to him again, because he appeared at the kitchen door only seconds later, just as she was pouring the glass of milk Kirsty had asked for.

'Forgive the intrusion,' he said as Diane opened the door to him. He was not looking at her, he was instead looking over her shoulder, into the kitchen. 'I take it Kirsty's here?'

'Good morning to you, too, Mr Channing.' Diane spoke coolly with only a hint of sarcasm. 'So you're looking for your niece? I wasn't sure whether you'd run out of coffee or sugar or something.'

That brought his eyes to hers; they narrowed slightly as he surveyed her, sweeping over her face as if determined not to miss any detail now. '*Touché*,' he said unsmiling.

Diane turned away to hand Kirsty her milk. She bristled when she heard the man's, 'Leave that, Kirsty. We have to go to London, right now.'

'*London?*' The girl looked devastated. 'But——'

'No buts. Come along, either leave it or drink it quickly.'

Kirsty did neither, she was staring at him in defiance. 'No! I'm not going to London, I hate it in London! We're going to the beach, you promised——'

'I didn't promise anything, child. I said we'd go to the beach, *all being well.* That does not constitute a promise.'

'You said if it was sunny. Well, it is, so why are you going to London?'

'Because I have to, why else? There's a problem at the office and I have to sort it out. Now come on, hurry up with that—and don't worry, we'll be back here tonight and we'll go to the beach tomorrow.'

Diane stood back and said nothing as the argument went on. It was only when she saw the threat of tears in the child's eyes that she intervened. 'Mr Channing, if it would help matters, I'd be very glad to have Kirsty with me for the day. I'm planning on going to the beach myself.'

For several seconds he said nothing, which was not the case with Kirsty, who was enthusing loudly while her uncle looked long and hard at Diane, as if gauging whether she could be entrusted with the girl.

'It's up to you,' she said, piqued by his rudeness. What on earth did he think she was, a child-molester?

It was only when Kirsty said for the fourth time, 'Oh, *please* say yes, Uncle Dominik!' that he deigned to answer Diane.

'Are you sure?'

'That I'm going to the beach today?'

'That you don't mind looking after Kirsty,' he said

impatiently, knowing she had deliberately misunderstood him.

'I wouldn't have offered if I weren't sure,' she informed him coldly, wondering why he always managed to rub her up the wrong way. 'However,' she added, glancing at the dog, 'I'd rather not take Penny, because——'

'Fully understood.' He glanced at the animal and clicked his fingers, bringing her to heel. This was followed by a swift look at his watch and, finally, by his thanks. 'Well, thank you, Miss West. I'm very grateful to you. There's no knowing what sort of time I'll get back, so I'll give you a key to Rose Cottage. Kirsty will have to get her things together and I must leave now.'

He took a bunch of keys from his pocket, extracted one and put it on the draining board, issuing orders to his niece at the same time. 'You behave yourself today, madam. *All* day. Miss West will give me a full report later, so bear that in mind. Do not argue with her the way you argue with me, do you hear? Do as she tells you—and don't stay too long in the water. You ended up looking like a prune yesterday, a shivering prune at that.'

Diane couldn't help smiling, though she tried not to. A shivering prune! She took one look at Kirsty's now belligerent face and started laughing. 'A shivering prune, Mr Channing? Was it that bad?'

To her surprise he actually laughed, his dark brown eyes warming, crinkling at the corners. 'It was.' To her further surprise he went over to kiss his niece, to hug her and ruffle her hair. 'Bye-bye, squirt, see you later.'

Kirsty's lovely face was wreathed in smiles as he left. No sooner had the door closed than she said, 'I love Uncle Nik, even though he's very bossy and he thinks I'm a tomboy. I'm not really. And he loves me, too,' she added, as if wanting confirmation.

'I'm sure he does. Who wouldn't? You're a smasher.'

Her smile faded, her eyes shifting to her untouched glass of milk. 'It's a good job I have him. I don't know where I'd live otherwise.'

Diane tried not to show how the remark startled her, and tried to be casual. 'So you actually live with him?'

'My mother died.' The child was staring into the milk. 'And my father lives abroad. He doesn't care much for me, anyway. So I live with Uncle Nik, in London—which I hate.' She brightened suddenly. 'Still, I'll be going away to boarding-school next month, in Devon.'

Diane's next question came carefully. 'And you like the idea?'

'Oh, yes! I'll be sleeping in a dormitory with lots of other girls my age.'

'I take it you're an only child, Kirsty?'

'Yes. My—parents split up when I was very young.'

Like Bobby's, Diane thought. But at least Bobby had his mother, no matter what Annabel was or was not. He had a stepfather now, too, and a stepsister. Diane knew from experience what it was like to lose one's mother while still very young; it had happened to her when she was seven.

She looked at the blonde curls on Kirsty's bowed head and wondered whether she really did like the idea of going to boarding-school, or whether it was something her uncle had decided on for purely practical reasons. 'Well, your new school will get you away from London, at least.'

'And from Uncle Nik's housekeeper,' the girl put in, looking up and pulling a face. 'She's horrid. She isn't used to children, she keeps telling me so. She was only used to looking after Uncle Nik and she hates me. I've told him she hates me, but he doesn't believe me.'

'Kirsty! I'm sure you're exaggerating.'

'I am *not*! You know what she called me last week? A little bitch. You see? And that's swearing. I told Uncle Nik, but I don't think he believed me about that, either. He says I tell stories.'

'And do you?'

The girl blushed furiously. 'Well . . . sometimes. But that was true, honestly! And it was only because my room was untidy.'

It was quite a day for Diane. By the end of it, or what she thought would be the end of it, she was beginning to wonder how the 'dynamic' businessman, the bachelor businessman, coped with Kirsty Nolan. The girl chattered incessantly, but it wasn't that that bothered Diane, it was her underlying need for attention, masses of it. It was insecurity, and it was understandable in the circumstances. Kirsty needed attention and reassurance in abundance. To put it simply, she needed to be sure she was loved.

She never mentioned her mother again, not in any context, which to Diane was an unhealthy sign. She didn't mention her father, either; instead it was Uncle Nik this and Uncle Nik that for most of the day. By four in the afternoon, Diane felt she knew the man very well. She was quite wrong about that.

He was not back at Rose Cottage when they got there. Diane rang the bell just in case, before letting herself in with the key, at which point it was getting on for five.

'He might not come back till midnight, you know.' Kirsty's warning came matter-of-factly. 'He might stay in London and have dinner with one of his girlfriends. He has lots of them—hundreds, in fact.'

Diane sank into a chair and kicked off her sandals. A few

grains of sand fell on to the carpet. Letting her eyes close, she thought before she spoke. Hundreds of girlfriends? With his looks and, no doubt, with his money, this particular revelation came as no surprise at all. Well, she couldn't care less about the man's love-life, but what she did care about was being exploited. Surely he wouldn't take off on a date? Not when he had left his niece with her? Not, at least, without so much as a telephone call?

By five-thirty she was beginning to wonder. Kirsty was complaining that she was hungry again, and Diane had to admit to feeling peckish in spite of a fairly substantial lunch.

'OK, let's take a look in the cupboards.' Diane hauled herself to her feet and wondered which she wanted most first, a meal or a bath. She felt gritty and sticky from the day on the beach.

The cupboards were bare. There was half a packet of cornflakes and three eggs in the kitchen; those and two pints of milk, a jar of coffee and some tea-bags, made up the entire contents of the cupboards and the refrigerator.

'We've been eating out,' Kirsty said helpfully, laughing at the disbelief on Diane's face. 'I told you Uncle Nik has a housekeeper. She does all the shopping and cooking. He hasn't got a clue about cooking anything—not even an egg,' she added, going into a giggling fit. 'We'll have to go to the supermarket, Diane, unless you want to eat out.'

The last thing Diane wanted was to eat out tonight, all she wanted was to relax. 'We will not have to go to the supermarket and we most certainly will not eat out. We will go next door and bring the makings of a meal back here. *I* have groceries.'

They trooped next door and raided the fridge, returning to Rose Cottage with the makings of a lamb stew which

seemed quite inappropriate for such a hot day. Kirsty had
eyed the packet of lamb chops and had put in a special
request.

'Pressure cooker or no pressure cooker, Kirsty, I warn
you it'll be at least an hour before you sit down to eat a lamb
stew.'

'I'll peel the potatoes and carrots—if you do the onions.
Honestly, it's nice made in a pressure cooker. My
mother——'

The sentence was never finished. Diane smiled and
argued no further; she only hoped the stew would turn out
as Kirsty's mother used to make it.

Whether it did or not, she had no way of knowing, she
merely watched with satisfaction as Kirsty wolfed her
helping down, and when she insisted on washing up Diane
let her. If Dominik's housekeeper was a tyrant, maybe she
didn't let the girl do anything in the kitchen, and maybe
Kirsty missed that? Her life now had to be drastically
different from her life with her mother—just her and her
mother.

By seven o'clock Diane was beginning to think very
harshly indeed of 'Uncle Nik'. He had, it really looked as if
he had taken himself off somewhere. There was no sign of
him, not even so much as a phone call, and what the hell
did he think he was doing? It certainly wasn't something in
the office, not at this time. So he thought he had a built-in
baby-sitter, did he? A sitting duck. It wasn't that she
minded keeping an eye on his niece, it was the principle of
the matter.

'Kirsty, let's go back to my cottage, I'm quite desperate to
have a bath. I'll be quick about it, you can watch telly for a
bit. OK?'

'But what about Uncle Nik? I mean, if he does come

back.'

'He'll know where to find us. Come on.'

He found the girls watching television in his own cottage. They got back there around eight o'clock—and he materialised at eight-fifty, apologising.

That he looked very tired was something Diane was determined to ignore; that his dark good looks were tensed with whatever he had on his mind was just too bad. However, for Kirsty's sake she toned down what she wanted to say to him. 'I'd given you up, Mr Channing. I thought you'd decided to stay the night in London.'

He looked at her as if she were mad. 'You're not serious? You mean——'

'I mean I think a telephone call would have been in order, don't you? To warn me how late you'd be? There's really no excuse for not ringing, especially when you've got a phone in your car.'

His eyebrows rose slightly and he shot a look at his niece, who was watching with amusement. 'Bed.' That was all he said to her, just the one word, but it was spoken in such a way that the child knew there was no room for argument this time. She tried, though, reminding him that she was on school holidays and that in any case it was only nine o'clock.

'I'm well aware of the time,' he told her, flinging his briefcase on to an armchair and glancing at Diane, who was wondering whether he always went into his office wearing denims. 'Bed, Kirsty. *Now*. And don't forget to brush your teeth first. Say goodnight and thank you to Miss West.'

When the child had left the room, with Penny on her heels, Diane got up to leave. 'I'll say goodnight, Mr Channing.'

'Just a minute.' Wearily he lowered himself into a chair,

gesturing that she should sit down again. She remained standing. 'I did ring you, Diane. You don't mind if I call you Diane? I rang around five-thirty and again around—I think it must have been about seven. Then I rang again when I was driving back, getting on for eight o'clock, I suppose. There was no answer each time.'

It was because he looked at a loss to understand this himself that she believed him. 'I—well, that was just bad timing.' She explained how she and Kirsty had spent an hour next door and, earlier, how they'd gone there to get some food.

'You mean you cooked her a meal? Please sit down—and do take that disapproving look off your face. I warned you this morning I couldn't tell you when I'd get back, and I did ring you three times, so what more can I say?'

'Nothing, I—sorry. I misjudged you, I thought you'd deliberately taken liberties.' She sat down again, feeling very awkward when she saw him looking at her carefully, as if really seeing her for the first time.

Quietly he said, 'I have the feeling we've both been guilty of that. I think we've both been misjudging each other since the moment I opened the front door to you the other night.'

Diane held his look, trying to see beyond the mere beauty of his eyes to discover what was really there, what he was really thinking. 'You might be right.'

He smiled; it chased away the tension in his face and transformed it, making her want to look away because she was sensing danger again, just as she had on their first encounter, that alluring but dangerous . . . something about him.

'And,' he went on, still smiling, 'now you've had an entire day of Kirsty feeding you information about me, as I know for certain she will have, you'll be convinced I'm an ogre.'

Diane laughed delightedly, shaking her head, causing her newly washed hair to swish around her shoulders. 'Absolutely not. She's crazy about you; she seems to think you're the best thing since chewing-gum.'

Dominik Channing hooted at that, to her further delight. 'I'm not sure I like the comparison, but you're right, she loves me every bit as much as I love her—but she complains about me all the time.'

'And you,' Diane said, realising this only now, 'are having a tough time of it with her, aren't you, Mr Channing?'

He shrugged. 'Dominik, please. Or Nik, if you prefer.' He got up to open a cupboard on a far wall. It was very well-stocked and Diane remarked on it.

'I see your bar isn't neglected the way your kitchen cupboards are. What did you think you could make from half a packet of cornflakes and three eggs?'

He turned to look at her, smiling again. 'A cornflake omelette?'

Whatever else he was lacking, Dominik at least had a sense of humour. Diane was laughing again. 'Well, between us Kirsty and I made a lamb stew and we saved some for you. I could heat it up and——'

'No, no, please don't bother. Thank you for the thought,' he added deliberately, 'it was very kind of you to cook for her and to think of me, but I'm not hungry. I'm ready for a drink. So what will you have, Diane?'

'Not for me, thank you. I must go.'

He turned to look at her again, the bottle of Scotch he'd picked up suspended in mid-air. 'Why must you?'

It was there again, that significance he sometimes injected into his words; he had asked the question as if to say he knew she didn't really have to go, as if to say that she herself should think about this. And he was right, there was no 'must' involved, she was free to do anything she wanted to.

'I'll have a gin and tonic, please.'

Dominik gave her a nod of approval before turning back to pour the drinks. He put her glass on a table beside her, offering ice, which she refused. 'Now, if you'll just excuse me for two minutes, Diane, I have a nightly ritual to perform—tucking Kirsty up. If I don't, she'll be shouting down to me in no time.'

'When did her mother die?' Diane asked the question as soon as he came back.

'In January.'

'Last January?' So it was that recent, just seven months ago. 'I hadn't realised; she's only mentioned her mother once today, to tell me she had died.'

He didn't seem surprised. 'I know, and that's bad, don't you think? I encourage her to talk about Jane—who was my sister, by the way, but she won't. Either she just shakes her head or she bursts into tears. She's bottling the whole thing up. I know she's suffering, but I don't know what the hell to do about it.'

And he *was* having a difficult time; he might have shrugged off her earlier remark about that but it was obvious. 'What was happening the other night, when I called for the key? Was she having a nightmare?'

'Yes. How did you know—or is that a stupid question? I really have very little experience with children myself. In fact, Kirsty is the only experience I have had, knowing her from the days she was born, I mean.' He looked up suddenly, his attention shifting from his glass back to Diane. 'I want to apologise about the other night, by the way. I was very curt with you, I know, but I was distracted and——'

'Forget it.' She spoke softly, meaning it; they had misjudged one another and she was glad of this opportunity to clear up their misunderstandings. There was nothing at all arrogant about Dominik Channing, he was not in love with himself and he was by no means as cocksure as she had thought. What he was like as a businessman she had no way of knowing, but, as a family man, if she could call him that, he was as vulnerable as anyone else. More so, because the care of his niece had been thrust upon him.

'There's no need for apology. I gave you the wrong impression, too. I'm not antisocial . . . in spite of what Kirsty told you about my not wishing to talk to you!'

His smile was back. Diane took a sip of her drink and looked away, half wishing herself elsewhere, half wishing she was not making these discoveries about her neighbour. This, while at the same time she knew she had a lot to talk to him about. She could help him, she knew, by telling him of her own experience, of the way her mind had worked after her own mother's death. She, too, had had nightmares; she had given her father a hard time for a long while. She looked back at Dominik and plunged in, telling him all about it.

He listened intently, interestedly, saying nothing until she had finished. 'The hardest part,' he told her at length, 'is answering all her questions. Without mentioning her mother, she still manages to ask me where people go when they die, why they die, why some die when they're young and so on.'

Diane nodded sympathetically. 'The best thing you can do is be honest, tell her according to your own beliefs.'

'I do. I tell her that God has a reason for everything, even though we don't always understand it. Another drink?'

He got up to take the glass from her and she forgot herself, forgot completely what it felt like to be touched by him in even the smallest way. When his fingers brushed against hers she felt that same shock, that same leaping of—of something she would rather remained dormant. Though it was the last thing she wanted to do, she found herself looking up at him quickly, wondering whether he had felt it, too. If he had, like the last time, he gave no sign of it.

'I've gone as far as thinking about taking Kirsty to a child psychologist,' he was saying, 'because of these nightmares. What do you think?'

'I wouldn't bother. She doesn't need a psychologist, she's behaving normally enough. All she needs is love and reassurance, and I don't doubt for one second that she's getting it from you.'

'Really?' There was amusement in the brown eyes now—amusement, warmth and . . . and a hint of wickedness? 'What makes you so sure?'

'Because beneath your tough veneer, Dominik, you are a caring and sensitive man.'

He roared with laughter at that; his head went back and he laughed so fully, he might well have been heard next door. 'That's precious! That is precious! Ah, if my business associates had heard you say that, they'd swear you should be certified.'

Diane shrugged. 'But I didn't meet you in a business setting, so I've glimpsed the real you.' Oddly enough, while she was going on to acknowledge that she had done only that, had only *glimpsed* the real Dominik Channing, he turned to look at her—and there was no amusement this time.

'But only glimpsed. You don't begin to know me, Diane, so don't make the mistake of thinking you do.'

Privately, she responded to that almost perversely, as if

he had challenged her to discover more. He hadn't, but her curiosity had been aroused and she was no longer half wishing herself elsewhere. She found herself wanting to know more, to know him more, even though there was that feeling of danger in the air again.

She did not reach for the glass he'd refilled, she was content for him to put it on the table beside her. 'What about Kirsty's father? She mentioned that he lives abroad and I found that puzzling. I didn't want to pursue it because she also said he didn't care for her much. Is that true?'

'It is and it isn't.' Dominik sighed, his fingers reaching up to push the thick black hair away from his forehead. It had a habit of falling forward, Diane had noticed. Irritated with herself, she looked down at the carpet. There was really no point in wondering whether his hair would be as pleasing to the touch as it was to the eye, no point in wondering what it would feel like to run her own fingers through it.

'Philip Nolan and my sister Jane got married because they had to,' he went on tiredly.

'Had to? In this day and age?'

He bowed his head slightly. 'Point taken. As far as Jane was concerned, they didn't have to. After the initial shock of finding herself pregnant, she told me she didn't love Philip enough to marry him.' He stopped talking abruptly, as if surprised at himself. 'Diane, why am I telling you all this?'

She was quiet for a moment, just looking at him. 'I don't know. Because I asked?'

He grinned at that. 'No. Because it's good to have someone to talk to, I mean someone objective. Someone who really listens,' he added, with a look of appreciation which pleased her to a ridiculous degree.

'Where was I? Oh, yes, my very strong-minded sister. Well, Jane turned out to be delighted at the prospect of having a baby. This, while our parents were horrified, and I mean horrified, because she had got herself into trouble. Those were their words, "got herself into trouble". They were old, with very old-fashioned ideas of right and wrong, proper and improper. They had me and Jane quite late in life, after trying for years and years.'

'Were? They're no longer with us?'

'No.'

'So—they put pressure on Jane to marry?'

'Enormous pressure, emotional pressure. And so did Philip. You see, the difference was that he was in love with Jane, I mean the madly-in-love, head-over-heels variety. Unfortunately, it couldn't last.'

'Why not? Do you mean it wasn't real?'

'Of course it wasn't real, it proved to be nothing more than infatuation on his part. My sister was extremely beautiful, you see.'

Diane looked at him and smiled in spite of herself. She had no trouble in believing how beautiful Dominik's sister had been!

'She also had a lot of personality,' he went on, smiling not at Diane but at the memory of his sister. 'She had character, I'll say that for her. She wanted to have the child and bring it up on her own, without the respectable cover of marriage. My parents freaked out at the prospect, you can imagine. As for Philip—well, he worked on her from his own point of view. I can't call it emotional blackmail, that would be inaccurate because he really believed he was in love with her at the time, no matter what the truth proved to be. In essence he told her it would be unfair of her to deny him the pleasure of his own child, of seeing the baby on a day-to-day basis. In the end, she suggested she live with him, which was another dreadful prospect as far as our parents were concerned, so to cut a long story short she did marry him eventually.'

'You can't cut it that short!' Diane protested. 'I'm hooked—what happened in the end?' No sooner was the question out than she was wishing she had worded it differently. She knew what had happened in the end . . . Jane had taken the ultimate exit from this story seven months ago.

'Philip's novelty with Jane wore off, so did the novelty of fatherhood. He was—is—an oddball in any case. He's a musician.' He paused, as if the explanation of Philip's being a musician should convey a great deal in itself.

'Not all musicians are oddballs, as you put it.'

'They are in my experience, though I confess it's a limited experience. Anyhow, he's a guitarist—classical, solo—and he admitted he had wanderlust. And his work took him away from home a lot. When he and Jane split they were both relieved about it and, of recent years, Philip has worked on ocean-going liners. He's travelled the world and at the moment he's under contract and working in the Bahamas. I don't know the details but he assures me he is under contract and that he would be sued if he were to break that contract. The truth might be that he doesn't want to, of course.'

'Or?'

'Or it might be that he is genuinely tied up.'

'Until when?'

'The end of the year, he says. Another four, five months.'

'And then what?' Diane shifted in her chair. Without noticing, she had slipped off her sandals earlier and she tucked her legs under her now, making herself more comfortable. The movement brought Dominik's attention to her legs and she flushed slightly, wishing she had left them where they were. She had changed into a bright red cotton skirt and top after her bath, and she pulled the material of the full skirt around her now. The last thing she wanted was another misunderstanding with Dominik. 'You were saying?' she prompted him. 'About Philip and his contract. What plans does he have when it's finished?'

In the face of his silence she was compelled to look at him again. She found him watching her oddly, as if she had said something out of context, as if she had quite suddenly changed the subject or something. 'Dominik?'

He grinned, and this time there was no mistake about the wickedness in his eyes. 'Excuse me. A slight distraction there. I find it very curious how the female body can be so much more fascinating when it's clothed rather than naked.'

She laughed deliberately. 'Now there's a *non sequitur* if ever I heard one!'

'Now when I saw you in your bikini yesterday, it was a delicious experience. I thought——'

'Dominik——'

'I thought your body, and I mean you in your entirety, beautiful. Very beautiful. Why are you looking at me like that? Do you think I don't mean it?'

'I think it irrelevant,' Diane said firmly, hoping she looked appropriately disapproving. 'You've digressed, to say the least.'

He was not put off, he was amused. 'You've got that stern look on your face, as you had earlier. Is that the best you can do when you're irritated? It's really very funny. My head-mistress in junior school used to look at me like that, I remember it as if it were yesterday. It was always the same face, the same expression.'

'And you really have disgressed.' It was lame, but she didn't know what else to say to bring him back to their earlier topic.

'You're right,' he agreed, becoming serious again. 'I was saying how beautiful I thought you, seeing you in that pink bikini, that *tiny* pink bikini, but there's still something mysterious about——'

'Look,' Diane cut in, 'just do me a favour, will you?' She could not allow this to go on, flattering and nice to hear though it was. There were too many other factors that prohibited this . . . flirting, if that was what it was. If she were to show her real response to what she was hearing, he could so easily misunderstand. She was sitting here in his cottage, drinking with him and talking with him, solely because of Kirsty. That was, it was owing to Kirsty that it had come about. She knew that and he knew that, but for all she knew, if she reacted to the way he was now talking to her, he might think she had been angling to get to know him all along, that she had merely used his niece as the means by which to do it. Well, that was not the case, not the truth, and she did *not* want him to think that.

'Do me a favour and get back to the original point,' she went on. 'I'd like to know what Philip plans to do when his contract finishes at the end of the year. About his daughter, I mean.'

'I know what you mean,' he said, gently, giving her the impression that he was laughing inwardly. Laughing at her . . . because he had an inkling of what was going through her mind? 'What's the matter, Diane? Why should you become unhinged just because I'm telling you you're beautiful, that your body is superb?'

Superb? There was no way she would describe it as such.

It wasn't half bad, that was all; he was going over the top and there was no doubt about it now, he was flirting with her all right. He was also grinning again, which annoyed her. 'I am *not* unhinged,' she said icily. 'I am merely disappointed. I can see it's time for me to go.'

'Wait a minute! All right, all right.' He held up a hand, unsure of her now, his eyes narrowing to probe the clear green depths of her own. 'Stay. Please. If I overstepped the mark, I apologise.'

'You did.' Diane didn't smile, but she did incline her head gracefully. 'And I accept your apology.'

There was a momentary silence as he continued to survey her. 'I'm curious about you, Diane. I was from the start. You're here alone at the cottage, and although you've stopped giving off those unfriendly signals and I've realised you're not as aloof as I'd thought, you are "defended". Very much so. So tell me, was my first impression of you right, after all? Are you basically a man-hater?'

This was so unexpected, so far off-target that she couldn't help laughing. 'A man-hater? Is that what you thought? Oh, dear! No, not at all. Why should I be?' It was her turn to hold up a hand. 'OK, OK, don't even try to answer that. I could be, couldn't I, for any number of reasons? But I'm not.'

'You just happen to disapprove of me?'

'No! Why should you think that? I had misjudged you, but I thought we'd got over that, cleared it up.'

'I thought so, too. Then what is it? Why do you refuse to listen when I'm talking about you, you rather than Kirsty? Why do I get the impression you resent my compliments?'

'I . . .' She felt foolish. Compliments. Was it that simple? Was she reading too much into the things he'd been saying to her? 'I'm sorry, I . . . perhaps I was ungracious. Perhaps

I should just say thank you, kind sir.' She added that with a smile, still feeling foolish and, something she was not, gauche. 'It's just that—I thought you were flirting with me.'

Dominik looked delighted. This, and more amused than ever. He was having difficulty not laughing aloud, she just knew it. 'But I was flirting with you. So what? Do you see what I mean about being "defended"? I *was* flirting with you—is that so terrible?'

It made things worse. He was absolutely right, of course, but did he have to be so blunt, so—so matter-of-fact? Exasperated, she wondered about the effect he was having on her, about the way she was tongue-tied now, having no idea what to say, no idea how to react.

It was as if Nik read her mind. 'Why don't you try being honest?'

'What? I . . . don't know what you mean.'

'I mean in your reactions. There isn't a woman on earth who doesn't enjoy being told she's beautiful, even if she doesn't think so herself. And you don't, do you? You have a poor self-image and that's a pity.'

'It isn't, because it isn't the case.' Nor was it, but she still wasn't being honest in her reactions, either. He had been quite right about that, at least. 'OK, thank you for your compliments, Dominik, and no, it isn't terrible if you were flirting with me.'

'Or if I still am?'

Diane looked straight into the warm depths of his eyes, smiling because they were smiling. For seconds nothing was said, not with words, but an understanding established itself and she acknowledged it. 'All right, Nik, if you want honest reactions, then that's what you'll get.'

'Splendid!' He then did something which left her open-mouthed. He got up and crossed over to her, picked up her left hand and pressed his lips to the back of it. 'It's very nice to know you, Diane West,' he said, 'and I look forward to discovering more.'

CHAPTER THREE

ALL Diane could think was that he had only had two drinks. So what was this? Was he sending her up, or did he normally behave like this? What man went in for hand-kissing these days? Worse, why was she secretly so pleased by the gesture? Was she basically a romantic or something? She had never, ever thought of herself as such.

Much later, she was to wonder about the look on her face. What had she looked like? Not that it bore thinking about, really, because, for all she knew, every bit of the shock she felt might have been showing all over her face.

And it was a shock, in the moment when, beyond the questions she had just put to herself, there was also that enormous physical pull towards him, towards him and yet away from him at the same time. She wanted to pull her hand from his and it was all she could do not to, all she could do to withstand his touch as he continued to hold her hand for a moment. When he did let go of her to return to his armchair, she stared at his back and acknowledged again that she had indeed had only a glimpse of this man earlier. Getting to know *him* was more than interesting, and she was more than curious now. She was undeniably intrigued.

'Philip,' he said suddenly, making her wonder for a moment who Philip was, 'is very much an unknown quantity.'

She smiled inwardly. Philip was an unknown quantity? She could say the same thing about Dominik, most definitely! 'In what respect?' she managed, finding difficulty in dragging her mind back to their earlier conversation. She had to shake herself mentally, to remember how and why this evening had come about, exactly. 'I take it you've been communicating with him, so what are his plans when his contract's run out?'

Dominik looked doubtful. 'He says he's coming back to England, he says he's going to buy a house and he's going to finish the job of bringing his daughter up. He says.'

'You don't believe him?'

He thought about that, seemingly careful with his answer. 'I don't know the man he is today; I'm influenced by the man I knew years ago.'

'But he might have changed, changed drastically. He might have satisfied his wanderlust and be ready to settle now. When did you last see him? Did he come back for Jane's funeral?'

'Of course.'

Of course? There was no 'of course' about it, was there? There was, it seemed, because Dominik added, 'And he was wonderful with Kirsty. He's never failed to write to her regularly over the years and he's talked to her on the telephone about once a month—from all over the world. He told her he would be back in the New Year, that he and she would make a nice home together. At that point, I saw the first hint of recovery in her, since before Jane's death, I mean. You see, it came as a surprise to no one; it was cancer and it was diagnosed as hopeless. Fortunately it was pretty quick, but we'd all had time to adjust, to accept what was going to happen. Kirsty had time to realise, really to know, that her mother was going to die.'

'Beware of that,' Diane warned him, closing her eyes briefly, aware of the irony of the similarity of the circumstances of Jane's illness and her own mother's.

Dominik seemed to know what she meant. 'No, it was genuine. Kirsty went into a decline several weeks before Jane left us. She's so much better now, believe me. Anyhow, her father helped enormously by telling her he was coming back to take over, and so on.'

'Then what's the problem? Why are you so dubious?'

'Because he suggested she began at boarding-school this year. I mean next month.'

Diane nodded. 'But she likes the idea, I mean, she really does. I sounded her out on that.'

There was another look of appreciation, the beginning of a smile which was just tugging at the corner of his mouth. 'Me, too. But I find that a happy coincidence and nothing more. From Philip's point of view, I understand his suggestion. He's a musician, which means he works during the evening mostly, so it would be difficult if Kirsty were at home. He pointed out to me that the choice was either her going to boarding-school or his employing a housekeeper full-time, someone who would look after her in the evenings.'

'Right. Seems reasonable to me so far. So why the dubiousness?'

Dominik got up, he was about to have a third drink and was looking questioningly at Diane. She shook her head; her glass was still half full and she could feel the effect of what she'd had in any case. Dominik's drinks were generous ones and she had to stay in control, absolutely in control. That sense of danger was still present, in spite of their having shifted back to neutral conversation. His very presence in the same room, it seemed to her, was unsettling. Or was that the gin talking? Come to think of it, what time was it? She took a surreptitious glance at her watch and found it was turned midnight. Unfortunately, Dominik turned to her just as she was reacting with surprise.

'Am I boring you, Diane? I'm sorry, I am going on and it really has nothing to do with you, it's just——'

'No!' She said it too hastily, too fervently, but it was already too late to worry about that. 'No, I asked, I am interested. Please go on.'

'There's little else to tell, really. I'll just have to wait and see.'

'Wait and see?'

'Philip, I mean. I'll have to see whether he does come back to England, whether he gets himself a home and—well, all of it. Only time will tell. But from Kirsty's point of view, there's safety. She has me.'

And if the look on his face was anything to go by, the child would never want for anything, least of all the love she so desperately needed. Dominik was clearly determined on that; she was his sister's child and he was her protector, no matter what her father did or did not do.

Something tugged at Diane's heart, a sympathy of sorts for Kirsty, probably. That the girl would be looked after, no matter what, she did not doubt for a second. The look of determination, of gravity, on Dominik's face told its own story. But he knew as well as Diane did that the love and protection of an uncle was not the same as the love and caring of a father. 'Dominik, I think you're being unfair on Philip.'

He looked at her swiftly with a mixture of interest and irritation. 'Really?'

'You're not giving him a chance.'

'Of course I'm giving him a chance,' he snapped. 'I know bloody well what the ideal is, whether Kirsty knows it or not. If her father comes through with his promises, she'll be far better off with him than with me. Because *he is* her father and I am not, and there we have it.' He said the last words with finality, as if Diane didn't fully understand.

She put him straight on that at once. 'I agree. Hey, if you're looking for an argument, pick another subject. You can give her everything she needs, including love, but you can't give her a father's love.'

It provoked a smile—more than that, it provoked raised eyebrows and a look of blatant admiration. 'You really are full of surprises, Miss West.'

'So are you, Mr Channing.'

There was another fleeting silence, another silent communication. Diane broke the silence, for she had a point to make and she was not going to be distracted from making it. 'You've already made up your mind about Philip Nolan. In spite of what you say, you aren't really giving him a chance. You've described him as an oddball, you've speculated about his wanderlust, but really you're convinced he won't be able to settle in one place, won't be able to make a proper home-base for his daughter. You are, as you've admitted, judging him on his actions in the past. Because he didn't really know his own mind then, because he didn't really know what he wanted when he married Jane, you think that's still the case with him. You're talking about more than eleven years, Dominik. You've changed in that time, and so has Philip. Who doesn't change in eleven years? You've said you'll wait and see, implying that you are prepared to give the man a chance to prove himself, but this in itself is arrogant in a way. Can you see that? So why don't you keep an open mind, why don't you really just wait and see, truly give him a chance?'

Nik wasn't merely looking at her, he was staring at her, and he did not look pleased. 'Oh, do go on! Why stop now?'

She intended to go on. 'Now who's being "defended"?

The point I really want to make is, how much have you coloured Kirsty's attitude towards her father and his plans with your own bias? Might you have countered Philip's positive input? You've told me he writes to her often—or at least regularly—that he rings her regularly, so why did she tell me that her father doesn't care much for her? The evidence seems to tell a different story. Why is that? Why didn't Kirsty even bother to mention to me that her father is coming home?'

Dominik shook his head slowly, he was raking his hair into place and looking at her with what she thought was anger. She was wrong in thinking that, she realised this when he got to his feet and started pacing around, moving from the fireplace to the doorway and back again. Eventually he picked up the briefcase he had thrown on to a chair and opened it, extracting a packet of long, slim cigars. Silently she watched as he lit one, his expression levelling into neutrality.

'You're right,' he said finally. He looked at her over the flame of his lighter, eyes narrowed. 'I suppose I might have influenced her unduly. Unwittingly. *Both*,' he added impatiently, showing that he was angry with himself rather than her.

Diane held up her hands, shrugging. 'It was a point worth making,' she said unapologetically. 'And now, Nik, I really must go.'

He was still on his feet, only one yard away from her as she stood. She could not know that her left leg, the one which had been under most of her weight, had gone to sleep. The moment she put it to the floor it buckled under her and she lost balance.

Dominik moved like lightning, his arm shooting out to provide something she could grasp, hold on to to steady herself. While she was muttering about her numb foot, he closed his hand around her wrist and turned to put his cigar down in an ashtray on the mantlepiece. And, while she was apologising and feeling foolish all over again, he didn't even hear what she was saying.

All Dominik saw was the glint of the light on her hair, blue-black silk he had the strong desire to touch. There was that and the look of bewilderment on her face, as though she didn't quite understand what had happened to her, a look of vulnerability he had glimpsed in her earlier. Impressions, fast and numerous, too many actually to register logically or detachedly. All he really knew was that she was half-way to being in his arms and that that was precisely where he wanted her, had wanted her to be for . . . he didn't know how long. Nor did he know how she would react, nor did he stop to think about it. He just gathered her close and brought his mouth down to hers, feeling yet again the incredible sparks which shot through him each and every time he touched her.

He had felt it from the start, he had felt it and recognised it and he had told himself he was extremely attracted to this girl . . . and so what? But this was different, he knew that now; as he kissed her, he knew this was an attraction unlike anything he had ever experienced before. Perhaps he was not as impervious as he had thought himself, after all. There had been many women, far more in the past than in recent years, the years during which he had become very choosy, very choosy indeed. He had thought of himself, at thirty-seven, as growing indifferent, or at least a bit jaded in some aspects of life, had thought himself incapable of being surprised by women any more.

He had been quite wrong about that.

When Diane wrenched away from him and slapped his

face with everything she had in her, Dominik really didn't
know whether to laugh or whether to take her seriously.
'Diane! What the——'

Diane was panic-stricken, appalled by what she had just
done. This had been more than she could handle. The
entire evening had been full of surprises of one kind or
another, shocks even, but this was too much. And it wasn't
over yet; no matter how much she wanted to escape from
Dominik, to run away from him, she was here in the
present and she herself was horrified at her behaviour. She
had slapped him, though she could hardly believe she had
acted with such violence, such drama. Yet even as she stood,
she saw the flush of red on his cheek as his skin reacted.
'Oh, damn! I—I'm sorry. I'm so sorry, Nik!'

So was Nik, but for different reasons. 'Just take it easy.'
He was not prepared to let her go, he was holding her in the
circle of his arms and he was damned if he would release
her. 'What was all that about?'

She wasn't looking at him and, when she said she didn't
know, he probed further, not willing to let it go at that.
'Diane, why so angry? I kissed you, that's all. I mean, I
kissed you, so what? I *kissed* you, I didn't commit a crime.'

'I—yes.' He was right, of course, she had to put this into
perspective. He had kissed her, that was all.

Well . . . it might have been 'all' to him, but to her it was
much more than that. She had been kissed by many men,
kissed and rather more, but she did not have enough
experience, or perhaps the right kind of experience, to know
how to handle this sort of attraction, one of such intensity.
The physical pull towards Dominik made itself felt all the
time, it had all evening, regardless of their serious conversation; it was as though it had an existence all its own. It
seemed to be independent of what was actually taking place

between them and yet . . . and yet the ease with which they had communicated, and the way that had pleased her, had served to add to it.

'Well, Diane? You said earlier that, since I wanted honest reactions, that was what I would get.'

She made herself look at him, ill at ease not only because she was still within the embrace of his arms but also because she couldn't quite come to grips with what was happening. 'Please let go of me.'

'No. Not yet, not until you tell me what's going through your mind.'

She closed her eyes, unable to withstand the probing of his, the way he seemed to be looking into her rather than at her. 'It's—nothing.'

There was low laughter, a soft sound which made her heart leap with renewed life. It was altogether too heady, being this close to him, so close she could feel the warmth of his body, could catch the all-male scent of him, the vaguest hint of the aftershave or cologne he had put on that morning. 'You're lying,' he said softly. 'An intelligent girl like you? There can't be a time when there's nothing going through that mind of yours. So why the historionics?'

In the face of her silence he ventured to answer the question for her. 'You want me, and what happened when I kissed you made it impossible for you to ignore it. Right?'

That got a reaction. 'Wrong!' She opened her eyes to glare at him. 'My goodness! You really do fancy yourself, don't you? I knew it the moment I clapped eyes on you!'

Dominik merely smiled, unmoved by her outburst. 'Is that what you knew when you first clapped eyes on me? Really, Diane? Well, I had quite a different experience: I took one look at you and thought you the most attractive woman I'd seen in a long time. Just my type—physically.'

He added the last word deliberately, grinning as he went on. 'But that was as far as it went. Putting matters physical aside, I thought you quite scatty.'

She wanted to laugh. She wouldn't—but oh, it was difficult not to! He had spoken so bluntly, so guilelessly, that if she didn't know better she would have thought him both tactless and clumsy when it came to handling women. But he was far from that, he was masterful, he had aimed and hit target twice in two of her most vulnerable areas, her innate sense of honesty and her sense of humour. She started to laugh—and Dominik moved in to take full advantage.

'Nik——' It was as far as she got, the smallest protest which had no chance to gain momentum, and so no chance at all of preventing him kissing her again.

As his mouth made contact with hers she was still protesting mentally. This, while at the same time her body yielded when his arms closed more tightly around her and pulled her close. Beneath the pressure of his lips her mouth yielded, too, allowing the kiss to deepen until it became an unhesitating exploration of her, a probing, a seeking of the response she was powerless to deny him. There was no longer any protest in her; this was not Diane thinking, not Diane as she normally behaved with a man. This was Diane reacting with total honesty, with an assertiveness she had not known she possessed. She kissed him back, wanting to taste and to discover in turn. Her hands had slid around his back and she was urging his body closer, revelling in the sensation of hard muscle against the softness of her breasts.

At the sudden sound of a dog barking, she started, stiffening in Dominik's arms.

'It's all right,' he assured her quickly. 'It's only Penny.'

She turned to look at the dog, but Penny was on the other

side of the closed living-room door and Dominik was making no move to open it, no move to let go of her. 'Listen to me,' he said, catching hold of her chin so she was obliged also to look at him. 'All she wants is to be let outside, just give me a moment.'

But as he moved towards the door Diane moved too, feeling grateful to Penny for this interruption. The animal stood in the hallway, wagging her tail, looking at the two humans expectantly.

'Is she yours or Kirsty's?'

'Kirsty's. When I inherited my niece I inherited her pet, too.' He grinned, opening the front door to let the dog out. 'And where do you think you're going, Diane?'

'I don't *think* I'm going anywhere,' she said. 'I *am* going home. I mean next door.'

They were standing in the open doorway. A slight drizzle was falling and the street outside was silent and still. Penny had vanished from sight, not that either of them noticed. Dominik reached for her, his hands closing around the bare flesh of her upper arms. 'Don't go yet, I'd like to talk to you more.'

'I'm sure you would,' she said drily, 'but I'm tired.'

'Wait a minute. I meant that—I meant talk.' He smiled at the look on her face, knowing and regretting what was going through her mind. 'You don't believe me. Well, I have news for you.' He spoke carefully, taking care also to look straight into her eyes. 'I'm not in the habit of saying one thing and meaning something quite different. Unlike some people . . .'

Diane groaned inwardly, cursing the way she reacted whenever he smiled like that, cursing the way he seemed to know her when in fact he knew nothing about her except the information Kirsty would have passed on, which was only basic. But he did seem to understand her very well on such a short acquaintance. Or was it just that he understood women in general? Yes, that was it. She wished she could feel angry at the idea, but she couldn't. 'Dominik, I really am tired. I mean it.'

He nodded reluctantly. 'I was forgetting, you've had a long day, and Kirsty during most of it.' He glanced heavenward, letting his hands drop from her arms. 'Heaven knows what an exhausting experience that can be! So OK, go to bed and sleep well. Perhaps we can finish this tomorrow.'

Now what did that mean, exactly? Diane found herself blushing as she hadn't blushed in years, hoping that the light from the living-room was such that he couldn't see it.

Dominik saw it and it amused him no end, but he wasn't going to let her know that, any of it. This woman, for all her twenty-four years, twenty-four according to his niece, was by no means as sophisticated as her attitude and appearance led one to believe at first glance. It had been a very long time since he had seen a woman blush like that, *caused* a woman to blush, a very long time indeed. But why the hell was he so pleased by it? 'Perhaps we can all go to the beach together,' he was saying, 'and, while Kirsty's building sandcastles or something, you and I can talk.'

'I'll—see how I feel in the morning.' There was no way she was going to commit herself to an outing. She was feeling idiotic again and was wondering at his ability to make her feel this way; it had happened several times during the course of this evening, and it was irritating to say the least. She was a successful, self-employed woman in her middle twenties and she should have outgrown this sort of reaction with people, male or female. It was just—him. Dominik, she had to face it, was out of her league. Maybe that was because he was some years older than she, ten at a guess, perhaps a bit more.

Nothing else was said apart from goodnight, at which point Dominik added his thanks to her both for her care of Kirsty and her listening to him.

Diane waved briefly as she got to the gate, turning towards Eden Cottage. The sight of Nik in the doorway, of his silhouette lit from behind, was something which went with her, however, and when she had brushed her teeth and pulled on a nightie she was still haunted by the image.

She climbed into bed and switched off the lamp at once. Reading for a while was out of the question tonight, for her mind was spinning with the events of the past few hours. Would she, if she'd had any idea of the way things would turn out, have made the offer this morning of looking after his niece for him? Well, there was no point in wondering about that, because what had happened had happened . . . and she was really making too much of Dominik's kissing her the first time. Thinking back to that, she cringed at the way she had over-reacted. She should have realised then, at that moment, that he was out of her league, far more than she was used to handling.

The memory of his second kiss was equally disturbing. No, it was more disturbing because her reaction then had been a revelation to her. There had been nothing withheld in those long moments, nothing at all gauche, or lacking, in her response to him. She had behaved like the woman she indeed was, every inch of it . . . but for the first time ever. Never before had she responded to a kiss with such passion, such fervour! It had taken Dominik Channing to draw that from her and—oh, lord—it had been so easy for him! He had handled the entire thing so very well—so cleverly, actually, reacting with no anger to her violence, seeing

straight through her denial of wanting him physically and
. . . and going on to prove his point superlatively well.

Sleep evaded her for over an hour. Learning more about
Dominik had also taught her a number of things she had
not known about herself. All in all, it was very
disconcerting, to the point where she wondered whether it
would be better, wiser, to avoid him from now on.

It was almost three in the morning when she finally
drifted off to sleep, and she only managed to do that
because she had reached a firm decision. When Kirsty came
around in the morning, as she inevitably would, Diane was
going to send a short but very clear message to Uncle
Dominik, a polite message, to the effect that she was not
available today.

CHAPTER FOUR

'KIRSTY tells me you're not available today.' It was almost ten o'clock and he was standing on the back doorstep because Diane was blocking his entry. 'Diane, in case you haven't noticed, it's pouring with rain and half of me is getting drenched. In other words, may I please come in?'

She stepped back, allowing him in because there was no way she could avoid it really. She might have known it wouldn't be an end to it, her sending Kirsty with the message. She gave Dominik a casual smile, shrugging. 'That's right, I have some thinking to do. I can't play out today.'

When he smiled in response to her last words it was like sunshine appearing in the kitchen. In reality it was a filthy day and nobody would be going to the beach, but there were lots of other things to do in a holiday area such as this.

'So why not think aloud? How about using me as a sounding board?' Without waiting to be asked, he sat at the kitchen table, surveying her openly from head to toe.

'Because what I have to think about is private.'

Either he ignored that or he really didn't hear her, she had no idea which; his eyes were still travelling over her but this time it didn't annoy her, did not make her self-conscious. In fact, she enjoyed his surveillance, actually felt confident about it. She had dressed very casually, but she knew that what she was wearing was flattering—from the male point of view, though when her father had first seen her wearing these jeans he had told her they were indecent.

That, of course, had been prior to his meeting Annabel, prior to his seeing *her* in similarly 'indecent' denims.

'This is grossly unfair of you,' Dominik was saying, his expression devoid of humour. 'Is there any water in the kettle? Boil it up and make me a coffee, would you?'

'What about Kirsty? Have you time for coffee?'

'Kirsty is under strict orders to stay put. Penny is with her and she knows where to find me if she really needs me.'

Diane turned round to switch on the kettle. It had boiled only minutes before Dominik had shown up. 'I'm sorry you feel it's unfair of me,' she said as she reached for mugs and the jar of coffee, 'but I really did come here to do some thinking.'

'I didn't mean that. Another spoon for me, please, I like it stronger than that. I was referring to those denims, Diane. Grossly unfair to the male population of Britain, especially with that T-shirt. And you're not wearing a bra.'

'I rarely do, unless I'm wearing something see-through.'

'So I noticed last night. Now then, about this thinking of yours. What's your problem?'

'I haven't got a problem.' Was that a lie? Yes and no; she had some adjustments to make, but she couldn't really describe that as a problem.

'Then come out to play. In view of the weather, I'm taking Kirsty to Compton House near Sherborne. Wouldn't you enjoy that?'

'I don't know what Compton House is.'

'It's a stately home, for one thing, and according to the brochure we've got, there's a "natural jungle" with "living exotic butterflies" there. That, of course, was the attraction for Kirsty. And there's a restaurant and whatnot. So what do you say? You don't really want to be stuck indoors alone all day, do you?'

It was precisely what she had wanted, or so she had thought. Now, though, turning to put Dominik's coffee on the table, she had a change of heart—and she knew why. She wanted to be with him, it was as simple as that. Whether it was wise or not was a different question . . .

'OK, Nik, I'm sold.'

He reacted with surprise. 'You are? I'm delighted!'

Diane was delighted, too, for she had expected him to say Kirsty would be pleased, not necessarily himself.

By eleven they were on their way to Sherborne in Dominik's dark red Mercedes saloon. Kirsty was on the back seat with Penny, who occupied more space than she did, and Diane was in the passenger seat next to Nik. Talking to him, however, was not practicable because Kirsty was nattering ten to the dozen in her usual fashion.

'Did I tell you I'm going to be eleven next week, Diane?'

'Yes, poppet, you did.'

'We can have a little party, can't we? Just the three of us. Oh, sorry, Penny, I mean the four of us! You'll still be here, won't you? You did tell me you're here for two weeks, like us?'

'I—think so.'

'You only think so?' Dominik turned to glance at her. 'You booked the cottage for two weeks.'

'Yes, but—well, I'll certainly be here for ten days if not the whole of next week. I'll be here for your birthday,' she added, turning to smile at Kirsty. 'That's on Wednesday, isn't it?'

'Mm. I'm a Leo, you know. What sign are you?'

'Taurus.'

'Uncle Nik's a Sagittarius, his birthday is the second of December.'

Diane turned to him, laughing. 'Sagittarius, eh? Oooh, that explains a lot!'

'Come on, it's the nicest sign of the Zodiac—whereas Taureans are stubborn.'

'Oh, yes? And what would you know?'

'His fiancée was very interested in astrology, wasn't she, Uncle Nik?'

He glanced heavenward. 'Is nothing sacred?'

'What do you mean?'

'Never mind, Kirsty, never mind.'

'Sagittarians,' Diane went on, grinning from ear to ear, 'have a healthy regard for the truth. They don't mind if it hurts, they would rather hear the truth than excuses or euphemisms or——'

'What's a euphemism?'

'Just a minute, Kirsty, I want to hear the rest of this. Do go on, Miss West.'

'I don't know any more—except that they like their freedom. So you got as far as being engaged, eh?'

Kirsty spoilt the game; she chipped in by reminding Diane that she already knew that bit of information. 'I told you, he was engaged but he decided he didn't like her in the end.'

'And that,' Nik said, taking his eyes from the road for what seemed like far too long to Diane, 'is precisely what happened. Satisfied?'

'Who asked?' she retorted, turning with much hauteur to look out of the window.

It was like that between them all day: there was a great deal of banter, of teasing, of laughter, much of which Kirsty was able to share. That Dominik was consistently light-hearted, consistently interested in what was happening around him no matter how trivial, surprised Diane. He had on his mind, to her certain knowledge, the matter of Kirsty and her father, and he had to be speculating as to the effect that Philip Nolan's behaviour would have on his, Dominik's, own life. Should Philip not 'come through', so to speak, then Nik's life would be permanently changed by the presence in it of his sister's daughter. Whether Kirsty was at boarding-school or not, there were school holidays and plenty of them, and possibly weekends at home when she got older.

'Do you live in a house in London, Nik?' she had asked at one point, when they were alone briefly.

He had looked at her blankly for a moment. 'Oh, I see, you mean as opposed to a flat or something. Yes, I have a house in Knightsbridge. I've got decorators in there at the moment, which is one reason Kirsty and I are down here. Another reason is that my housekeeper is on holiday for two weeks, and in any case Kirsty needed a break. She hates living in London. She's used to country life, you see. Jane lived just outside Ringwood in a rural area, not far from where we are in the cottages. Her house has been sold, of course; there was no point in keeping it on because Philip wouldn't want to live in that area. Jane used to do all the bookings for me—I think Kirsty's told you I have a number of properties here and there?'

'I'm afraid so.'

He had smiled. 'Well, the woman who's currently handling the bookings is incompetent, useless, as was the one before her, the one who took over from Jane. However, I'm very glad of this particular case of mismanagement,' he'd added, smiling straight into her eyes. 'Both Eden Cottage and Rose Cottage should have been occupied by two families who——'

'I told her all that, about the mix-up of dates.' Kirsty

had appeared from nowhere, behind them, and that had been the end of the conversation.

So Dominik had Kirsty and Philip and his business affairs on his mind, and who knew what else? But he was fun to be with, regardless, seemingly without a care in the world.

He was no different after his niece had been packed off to bed that night, either; the teasing continued even then. Diane waited until he had tucked the child up for the night, and when he came back to the living-room she got up to leave.

'Honestly,' he was saying as he came into the room, 'the *questions* that girl asks me! I—what's the matter, Diane? You're not going?'

'Yes, but not before I've thanked you for a lovely day.' She was smiling because it really had been a lovely day in spite of the weather, maybe even because of it. Had it not rained all day, or had it not been raining in the morning at least, she might have stuck to her guns and stayed alone, knowing there would have been the prospect of sun-bathing in the garden.

But it hadn't worked out like that. She, Kirsty and Nik had had dinner in the family restaurant down the road—at which point he had mentioned going somewhere 'a little different' the next day. He had said it without deference to her, so whether he was including her in his thinking or not she had no idea. Whether she would permit herself to be included she had no idea. She had decided much earlier just to play this thing by ear, which was what she was doing now. Or rather, it was what she thought she was doing.

In truth, she was about to make an excuse and plead a tiredness she was not actually feeling. She was all prepared to mention her late night last night and another long and very full day today, but she never got that far. Dominik wasn't going to miss this opportunity of teasing her, that much became obvious very quickly.

He was laughing at her now. 'What's the matter? Afraid to be alone with me? Perhaps you don't trust me.'

She answered without preamble. 'You're too right.'

'Well, good for you!' He went on to compliment her on this honest response, but that was not, as she might have known, going to be the end of it. 'Or maybe you don't trust yourself? Could that be the case?'

Fortunately she had seen the glint in his eyes, that wickedness she had come to recognise at once. It seemed to make things much simpler if she answered him honestly, so she did, again. 'Perhaps, Nik. Perhaps I don't trust either of us.'

'But why fight it?' He sprawled in an armchair, his head resting against the wing of it, his left ankle hooked over his right knee. Relaxed, totally at ease . . . and still taunting her.

'You wouldn't understand.' Diane bent to pick up her shoulder-bag, feeling the smile slipping from her lips. He wouldn't understand. How could he?

'Try me.' It was an invitation, not a challenge, but she didn't take him up on it in any case.

'Some other time, perhaps.'

To her surprise he let it go at that; he got to his feet to see her out, and it was only then that he took hold of her, but just in the most casual way, his arm coming out to touch her shoulder, to turn her round to face him fully. 'Diane, seriously, what is on your mind? What I mean is, can I help you?'

She opened her mouth and closed it again, shaking her head, knowing what was perhaps a disproportionate pleasure at his unmistakable sincerity. He was genuinely concerned, frowning now, his eyes seeming an even darker brown but still making a dramatic contrast to the jet-black of his lashes. That errant lock of hair had fallen over his forehead, but he let it be, not noticing even at an unconscious level.

Diane could do no more than look at him, at all of this. He really was beautiful! The small, poorly lit hallway was throwing shadows across his face, accentuating the planes of it, and she found herself studying his mouth, seeing in it the sensuality she knew from experience it was capable of. The desire to kiss him was not a sudden or unexpected one; she had felt it all day. To a greater or lesser extent she had felt it all day and, now, she no longer saw a reason to resist this temptation.

It took only the smallest movement for her to be close enough, to raise her head and touch her mouth against his, just lightly, just enough to satisfy without lingering long enough to create a further need. With Dominik, that would be far too dangerous. 'Goodnight,' she whispered, moving past him into the cool, damp evening.

The strangest thing happened to her then. She hadn't even reached the door of her cottage before she felt tears on her face. Stepping into the safety of privacy, she put her fingers to her cheeks, incredulous. Tears? But why? The entire day had been wonderful, the best she had spent in years, so why this? What on earth was wrong with her? What was she thinking about?

Nik, she was thinking about Dominik, of course. If she were honest with herself, which she was trying hard to be, she knew a sense of disappointment because he had let her go without argument. Was she crazy? It was only reasonable that he should, wasn't it? They had spent eleven solid hours together—why shouldn't he let her go when she had virtually insisted on his doing so?

In the cottage next door, sitting again in the armchair, Dominik found himself looking at the wall to his left. Diane was on the other side of that wall, only feet away from him, in fact. These cottages were small but their walls were thick; she might as well be several miles away for what difference it made. She had gone, taken her leave, and it was barely nine-thirty in the evening. Why? What was she going to do with herself until it was time to go to bed?

A wry smile came to his mouth. When he got into bed himself that night he would be thinking about her, imagining her in bed. Which room was she sleeping in, the twin or the double? The double; of course she would have opted for the double. What did she wear in bed, if anything? If she did wear something, it would be incredibly feminine, of that he could be sure. She was a very feminine female, though she had remarked to him today—he couldn't remember at what point or even the context—that she did not think of herself as being particularly feminine. She was wrong about that. Diane did have a poor self-image, he had been accurate in telling her so.

Mentally he shook himself and got up to pour a drink. With a generous amount of Scotch in his glass he settled down again, but it was no use, he was still thinking the kind of thoughts he had not entertained about a woman for years. Not even with Eve had there been this kind of intrigue, and nothing like the same physical attraction. Now there was a mystery. Why did he feel the way he felt about Diane West? Why was it so strong, even stronger now that it had been last night? Stronger the more he got to know her.

And what the hell was she afraid of? Why, when she felt it too, had she run away from him tonight? That was what it amounted to; he didn't believe for one minute that she had been motivated to go by something other than fear. Or was it merely a game? They had enjoyed their own games today, many of which had gone over Kirsty's young head—their banter, their teasing, their deliberate ambiguities, their flirting. No, not that, Kirsty had picked up on the flirting all right. Children, he reminded himself, picked up far more than adults ever gave them credit for. He recalled the question Kirsty had asked when he'd gone to tuck her up tonight. 'Why did you send me to bed early again? Do you want to kiss Diane, is that it?'

He laughed aloud now. Did he want to kiss Diane? He'd had every intention of kissing Diane—but Diane was playing hard to get. It was that, wasn't it? A game. He had given her the benefit of the doubt earlier, when he had thought her afraid for some reason; he'd let her go without argument because there was no way he was going to spoil this relationship by pushing things. He liked her. Quite apart from the physical attraction, he liked her very much.

His eyes moved back to the wall connecting the cottages. He was feeling uncertain now and he did not like the feeling.

Was she playing hard to get?

Or was she really hard to get?

Diane was trying to make a decision, one she would stick to. Should she call a halt now with Dominik, before things got out of hand, or should she simply let herself move with it, whatever it was, and let things take their course?

What exactly was it? Were they friends, she and Dominik? If they weren't, they certainly could be, for they got on well, irrespective of anything else. Now there was a euphemistic thought! She laughed aloud in the silence of her bedroom, wondering whether he had gone to bed yet.

No, better not to speculate on that, that was the 'anything else'. It was not and would not be the way it had been with the other males in her life. This, Dominik, was different. If she gave him the leeway she had allowed a few others, a very few others, it would be far too much; if she gave him an inch he would take a mile. To put it simply, with Nik it would be all or nothing, she knew that as certainly as she knew the sun would rise in the east tomorrow—whether it was visible through the clouds or not!

Her decision was already made, however; maybe it had been before she had even started to think things through. How could she resist being with him, how could she refuse when he asked her, as he surely would, to spend more time with him an Kirsty? With him and Kirsty. Thinking about that delightful little chatterbox provoked another thought, another point, and it was simply that the very presence of that child was a safeguard in many ways . . . a safeguard that she needed. Didn't she?

Impatient with herself, she turned over for the umpteenth time and wondered for the umpteenth time why she had to analyse things so much. Did other women do this? Of course they did, she knew they did. But to such an extent? No, not all women. There were some who would not be giving this episode a moment's thought. Well, hardly. She herself had girlfriends, at least two of them, whose attitude would be very different from her own. The two she had in mind, old friends from schooldays, would think her mad if they knew what she was going through right now. With the likes of Dominik Channing they would hurl themselves into an affair with barely a second thought.

So what was her hang-up? There wasn't one—not unless her own self-respect was a hang-up. That was what it boiled down to: she hardly knew the man. In spite of feeling she knew him quite well, she in fact did not. How could she, in so short a time?

This mattered; to her it mattered very much. Whether it might be regarded as old-fashioned by others or not, it was how she felt.

So the decision was made. Avoiding Dominik was unnecessary and definitely undesirable. But keeping him at arm's length was necessary and . . . well, it was necessary.

CHAPTER FIVE

DIANE was successful in keeping Dominik at arm's length. It was not easy, but for four days and three evenings she managed it. It was on the Saturday that things changed.

For the four days from Wednesday to Saturday, she, Dominik and Kirsty were together all the time—until around nine in the evening. At that point the day was over as far as Diane was concerned, and she took off for her own cottage. Dominik let her go without protest every time, giving her only a knowing smile which irritated her beyond words and at the same time made her more determined in her resolve.

It was during lunch on the Saturday that he told her he had organised a babysitter for that evening. The three of them together with Penny had trooped from the beach at Boscombe to have a pizza, which Kirsty said she particularly fancied.

'Who's babysitting me?' she wanted to know. 'And why?'

'Mrs Archer,' Dominik informed her, with a warning look.

'Mrs Archer! But she's—what did you call her? Incompetent. Yes, that was the word.'

'Given that she's managed to bring four children to adulthood, I'm sure she will not be incompetent as a babysitter.'

It was only then that Diane remembered who Mrs Archer was; the woman who did the bookings on the holiday properties. She had learned that these were not the major part of Nik's business, and that he was actually in the process of selling them off piece by piece, as he'd put it.

'As for your other question,' he was saying to Kirsty, 'the why of it, the answer to that is quite simple. I want to take Diane out to dinner, a grown-up dinner.'

Kirsty grinned very broadly at that. 'You mean you want to be alone with her.'

'Yes, I want to be alone with her.'

The child shot a quick look at Diane, who kept an impassive face until Kirsty added, 'I know, you want to wine her and dine her.'

'Kirsty——'

'I've read about that stuff, in books.'

Dominik shook his head, stifling a smile. 'Where else, darling child? Given that you've read about it, I didn't think you'd seen it written across the heavens.'

'It could have been in a magazine,' his niece pointed out, at which Diane started laughing and couldn't seem to stop.

'Between the two of you,' Nik said, looking only and very pointedly at Diane, 'what chance have I got?'

She leaned forward to dig him playfully in the ribs. 'Come on, Dominik, you can take that helpless look off your face, it doesn't wash with me!'

It wasn't quite true; she had seen that look at moments when it was genuine, when Kirsty would come out with something bordering on the outrageous, something requiring an answer she would have been hard pressed to provide herself. She sympathised with him, being flung into the surrogate fatherhood of a ten-year-old female. Well, almost eleven, but a girl who was young for her years.

It wasn't until later in the afternoon that Diane thought to ask Nik where he was taking her that evening. They were back on the beach, sitting on towels and watching Kirsty playing with some other children in the sea.

When there was no answer, she shifted her gaze to him, feeling her breath catch in her throat. It had happened several times today, this being the first time she had seen him without his clothes on, as good as naked as far as she was concerned. It was only today that the sun had made its reappearance in a serious way, which had enabled them to spend their time on the beach rather than driving around to find other attractions, not that that had presented a problem.

It was the combination of the way Dominik was looking at her as well as the way he looked that left her breathless. He was making no attempt to hide what was in his mind; he was letting his eyes trail over her in her pink bikini, her *tiny* pink bikini, and loving every minute of it. Tempted to say something flippant, something about there being more mystery in a fully clothed female body, she found she could not. It was not a moment for flippancy.

'We're having dinner at the Royal Bath Hotel in Bournemouth,' he said, and she could only nod and be grateful that, because clothes were her business, she never travelled anywhere without having covered all possible contingencies. She had an appropriate dress with her.

'That—sounds good.' She looked away, towards the children, feeling acutely aware of Nik and his near-naked body. He was, she thought, truly a magnificent specimen. In her opinion the whole of him was beautiful, his body no less than perfect, muscular but far from muscle-bound, lean but far from being thin. The obvious strength in it could make her feel weak if she dwelt on it for too long. The broadness of his chest, the movement of muscle beneath the hair on his thighs, the far more generous scattering of hair on his chest—none of it bore too much examination.

Dominik didn't have the same reluctance. Even as she kept her eyes on the children, and in particular on Kirsty, she could feel his eyes on her, could feel the response in her, too, as surely as if he were touching rather than looking. 'What time would you like me to be ready tonight?' she asked, still keeping her eyes front.

'Seven-thirty. Mrs Archer will come to me around seven-fifteen, so I'll come a-knocking at your door, OK?'

'Fine.'

Fine. Except that by seven o'clock she was as nervous as a cat, and being annoyed with herself because of it was senseless, didn't help in the least. Fortunately she had made-up before the nervousness set in, so that was satisfactory; it was what to wear that was worrying her now. The dress she had so quickly decided upon was . . . too seductive, altogether too seductive. At least, it would be to Dominik. She knew the way his mind worked: its low-cut bodice would keep his eyes from her face all evening, probably.

'You're being ridiculous.' She spoke aloud in an effort to break her train of thought. Her mind was leaping ahead, not really to the hours she would spend with him over dinner but to later, to what might happen later. 'Might, not will, Diane.' She spoke to her reflection firmly, reminding herself that she was in control of herself. She, not Nik, so what was she worrying about, really?

He rang her doorbell at seven-thirty on the dot, dressed in a lightweight grey suit, finely striped and immaculately cut. With it he wore a shirt of the palest blue and a tie several shades darker. It was the first time she had seen him dressed other than casually, but even so she should not have felt as impressed as she was.

It was a similar experience for Dominik. He took one

look at her and knew that the game had come to an end, that she had decided to stop playing hard to get. She was wearing a dress which had been designed with seduction in mind, a dress of shiny material as black as her hair. It was close-fitting, sleeveless, and there was very little of it at the front, and nothing, he discovered as she led the way into the living-room, nothing of it at all at the back, nothing to speak of, anyway, just the halter-neck he couldn't see under the length of her hair. And she smelled like a dream; he didn't know the name of the perfume, which was something he had taken a foolish and immature pride in when he was younger. It had amused him, in earlier days, to be able to name the perfume a woman was wearing.

'Nik?'

'What?' He hadn't heard what she'd just said; he had heard her speaking but had no idea what she had actually said. What was the matter with him? He couldn't take his eyes off her, and his thoughts had become insanely preoccupied.

'I was saying, I'm sorry I can't offer you a drink, but I didn't buy any——'

'That's OK, we'll have one in the bar when we get to the hotel. Let's go, Diane.'

She blinked in surprise at his abruptness, wondering what was going through his mind. He had said nothing about her appearance, there had been no compliment —except that which was in his eyes, so it wasn't that he disapproved of what she was wearing.

'Is something wrong?' She asked the question as soon as they got in his car, which he had brought round to the front of the cottages. It was sandwiched between Diane's car and what she supposed was Mrs Archer's. 'Kirsty wasn't playing up, was she? About your going out, I mean.'

'No, not at all. If she were to start playing up over something like that, I'd soon put a stop to it, believe me.'

Diane believed him. 'Then what is it? Your vibes are all wrong.'

It got a smile; as he shifted the gear lever into 'Drive' and pulled gently away from the kerb, he turned to look at her. 'You read me well, Diane. I'm impressed.'

She shrugged. 'I'm very sensitive to atmospheres and to people's moods, that's all.'

'You're right, too. My vibes are off, but it won't last, don't worry.'

Which meant he wasn't going to tell her what was on his mind. Well, she would not ask again. It was no big deal in any case, because within five minutes they were on the open road and communicating with one another as well as they always did. Whatever had been bothering Nik was now forgotten.

'So tell me, how did you come to be a manufacturer's agent? Was this something you'd planned to do?'

Diane laughed at that, shaking her head avidly. They were in the lounge bar at the Royal Bath Hotel, a gracious white building on the very edge of the south coast, enjoying luxurious surroundings and a scrupulously attentive service. She leaned forward to take a stuffed olive from the array of nibbles which had been placed before them, glancing up to admire again the gorgeous view across the bay. 'No, I was never particularly ambitious over anything. I left school at sixteen, spent a year at full-time secretarial college and got a job in the offices of the leatherwear manufacturer whose clothes I now sell. I have three agencies: the leatherwear, up-market knitwear which is really gorgeous, and I carry a range of furs. The furs are simulated, but again, better quality.'

'Does your territory include central London?'

'Yes, except for the leatherwear. My erstwhile boss is no fool; all the inner London customers are house accounts.'

'Your erstwhile boss?'

'He's the one who's responsible for my being on the road. Quite simply, when I worked in the offices at the factory, which is just outside Maidstone, I used to get hauled regularly into the showroom to try things on for customers.'

Dominik smiled. 'I can understand that; with a figure like yours I'm surprised you didn't go in for modelling.'

It was an idea which had never crossed Diane's mind. Her figure might be good, but professional modelling required more than that; it required a face equally good. 'Anyhow, I just found that I could sell. I seemed to say all the right things to customers, or so my boss was always telling me. Then one day he suggested I go on the road for him. At first I thought he was joking, but no. To cut a long story short, I ended up doing just that, working for a wage plus a small incentive commission.'

She broke off, laughing at how naïve she had been, laughing at the memory of those early weeks, now several years behind her. 'I was being exploited, Nik. I soon realised I would be better off working solely on a commission basis, on a proper percentage, I mean. I was very good at selling. I had a long conversation with my boss, who tried to talk me out of the idea, insisting I had more security with a wage. I told him he was a rogue; I told him he could take my offer or leave it because I was going to take on other agencies in any case.'

'So he took it.'

'He did indeed. We're the best of friends these days. He's very shrewd, but very nice with it.'

Rather like you, she added silently, before attempting to

change the subject. It wasn't that she minded talking about her work, it was just that she didn't want to bore Nik.

Dominik was far from bored, he wanted to know all there was to know about this woman. He encouraged her to talk about herself, and when they moved from the bar to the Garden Restaurant he observed with amusement the way she kept trying to change the subject.

When they had ordered their dinner, he tackled her about it. 'Why don't you like talking about yourself, Diane? Most people do, you know.'

'And I'm no exception,' she told him honestly. 'Of course I like talking about myself, who doesn't? But talking about my work can be boring to other people.'

'I am not,' he said, reaching for her hand, 'other people.'

Diane glanced around the room, knowing, just knowing, they had not been put at this corner table by chance. It was one of the best tables in the room—for those who did not wish to be overheard.

'Or am I?' he was saying. 'Is that all I am to you—another person?'

She looked at him, envying his confidence, a confidence she herself was not feeling. He knew very well that he was more than that to her. That he had become more, much more, within the space of only one week did not matter to her. She was no longer thinking in terms of time, she was wondering quite *what* Nik had become to her, exactly. Very casually, because she really did not know how to answer without giving herself away, she told him that, like her erstwhile boss, he too was very shrewd but very nice with it.

'A non-answer if ever I heard one.' Dominik let go of her hand and leaned back, as if to see her the better from a little distance. 'I want to know more.' He held up a hand, smiling at the look on her face. 'I don't mean I'm pushing you for an answer to my last question, I mean I want to know more about you. Tell me about this flat you're buying. Where is it?'

It turned out that Dominik knew the building, and she didn't have to tell him what the flat was like because he already knew that, too. 'How come you know all this?'

'It's my business to know these things, literally my business. I don't build from scratch, but I do buy properties and convert them into flats. That's mainly what my business is about. But,' he added, giving her that heart-stopping, all-knowing smile, 'if you think you've just succeeded in changing the subject, you can think again. You're pretty shrewd yourself, madam, but only in some respects. In others . . .'

'In others, what?'

'In other ways your innocence is yet another source of surprise to me. No, innocence is the wrong word . . .' He broke off, surveying her carefully, as openly as ever, letting his eyes take in all the details of her face, her hair, her bare shoulders—and pausing to linger just briefly on the swell of her breasts in the low-cut dress. 'Innocent, Diane, is something you are not. And yet . . .' Again he seemed to be having difficulty summing her up, and on the one hand it amused her, while on the other she felt slightly panicky.

Diane knew very well how capable she was of giving people the wrong impression; sometimes she did it deliberately. That she was not as wordly-wise and confident as she appeared to be was something only she and her father knew . . . or so she had thought. But Dominik knew it too, she felt sure of that. Perhaps he had been right in saying she had a poor self-image, although she had denied it at the time. Why *didn't* she think of herself in more positive terms? After all, she really was successful in her work;

people liked her both in and out of it . . . with very few exceptions.

The feeling of panic overrode her amusement when she saw Nik's eyes shifting back to her cleavage. She should not, she absolutely should not have worn this dress. Hadn't she known it was a mistake? Yes, but she had ignored that knowing and had worn it none the less. Talk about giving the wrong impression! It seemed perverse of her in retrospect, and it certainly *was* perverse of her to be feeling this sudden resentment of Nik. She became defensive. 'I have two things to say to you, Dominik. First I'd like to remind you that you broke off in mid-sentence, and secondly I'd like you to know that you are ogling me, and in public at that. It's offending me.'

That brought his attention back to her; he fixed her with his eyes, amused and very beautiful eyes. '*Offending* you?' He laughed aloud, seeming genuinely amused. 'Darling girl, what do you expect of me? I happen to be male, remember? A very normal, very healthy male. So if you're looking for an apology you'll be disappointed, because I'll be damned if I'm going to apologise for being attracted to you, for admiring you. That's all it is. So tell me, what's offensive about that?'

Diane wished she hadn't said anything. She was grateful for the interruption of the wine waiter with the wine Nik had ordered, immediately followed by another waiter with their first course. No matter what he said, she knew without doubt now that Nik was misunderstanding her. No, there was nothing wrong in his admiring her, his being attracted to her, it was just . . . just that he was misreading her and it was entirely her own fault.

Her eyes closed briefly. Dear lord, why did she have to be so complicated? Why couldn't she just simply be herself?

Why did she worry so much about what he was thinking?

'Diane?' The word came softly, and she looked up to find Dominik watching her with eyes so gentle, so obviously concerned about her, that she relaxed inwardly. 'You are,' he said, very quietly, 'an enigma to me. That I admit. I have so many different impressions of you, so many that I can't sort out the truth from my imaginings. I find myself knowing you and not knowing you, I find myself speculating and supposing . . . and hoping. Hoping, mainly, to know you, and I mean really know you.'

She looked down at her plate and decided that a long drink of wine was in order before she started eating. Something deep inside her was withdrawing from him, almost resenting him again, while at the same time she wanted to hear more. This, while at the same time, her body seemed to be yearning towards him . . . it made no sense at all. 'I—Nik, your soup's getting cold.'

This was met with a grunt, but he started eating and for minutes nothing was said. When next they spoke it was at his instigation, and they were once again on the subject of her, but not at such a disturbingly personal level.

'So you've been living at home, with your father. I hadn't realised that until you mentioned it yesterday; I'd assumed you were moving from one flat to another. It never occurred to me you'd been living with your father.'

Diane smiled and shrugged at the same time. 'I know, it's quite unusual to be leaving home at the age of twenty-four, isn't it?'

'I think so.' As far as Dominik was concerned, this only added to the mystery she represented. 'And why are you leaving home now? What exactly has prompted this?'

She glanced away, making a quick decision. She was not going to spoil this evening, this evening and the equilibrium she had only just gained, by talking about Annabel. Thinking about her stepmother was not something she wanted to do right now, not while she was with Nik. 'Oh, my father has remarried and it's not practicable for me to stay at home any longer.'

'Remarried? Good for him!'

She looked at him quickly. 'What makes you say that?'

He seemed surprised by the question. 'Well, he's been on his own all these years, hasn't he? Didn't you say you were seven when your mother died?'

'Yes,' she said, determined she *would* change the subject this time. 'I was seven. Which reminds me, has Kirsty had any more nightmares since the one last Saturday?'

'No.' Nik looked pleased at the idea and she thought her ploy had worked, but she was wrong. 'Diane, about you—is there a man in your life?'

'I—no, no there isn't.'

'Then has there been someone who—have you ever been close to marriage? Engaged?'

'No.'

'And why is that?'

'Dominik! That's an impossible question!' She laughed, emptying her wineglass and making no protest when a waiter appeared out of nowhere to refill it. A second bottle was ordered and she realised, without worrying about it, that it was she who had had most of the first bottle. Dominik was going very easy on the wine and he'd had only a glass of tonic water in the bar. 'That's just how it is,' she went on. 'And that's the simple answer to some questions, you know. It just *is*.'

He raised his glass as if in a toast to her, smiling but without any wickedness. 'All right, it just is.'

'On the other hand,' she said, knowing she had villainy in

her own eyes, 'with you it's a different story. You were engaged. So what happened?'

He took a moment to answer. Finally, determinedly non-committal, he said, 'Kirsty told you. I decided I didn't like her in the end. It was all a mistake.'

'Meaning I should mind my own business?'

'Meaning it's simply not worth talking about. I'd rather talk about you than about Eve.'

'Eve? Was—is that her name?'

'Very clever.' He tucked into the steak he had ordered to follow his soup. 'But that's as far as we go, Diane. Eve is her name, yes, but as far as I'm concerned, it *was* her name. As far as I'm concerned she doesn't exist any more.'

Which sounded positively unhealthy to Diane. If he were so determined to forget Eve, to the point where he regarded her as not existing any more, then he must have been deeply affected by her presence in his life. Maybe he was still in love with her. He was probably still in love with her. If his engagement to her had been merely a mistake, then why should *he* be so defensive, defensive to the extent of not wanting to talk about her, of wishing to blot her existence out of his thinking?

It was a depressing concept, realisation. That Nik was, whether he knew it or not—and he probably didn't—still in love with this woman was enough to send Diane into a whole new phase of analysing. Not that she realised this would be the effect on her; it would be later, much later, that she would find herself wondering about the woman called Eve.

Between that point and their leaving the restaurant, there was plenty happening to keep her mind occupied. When they left the hotel it was raining hard and Dominik told her to stay indoors. He brought the car as close to her as he could get it, and she got into the passenger seat, shivering, wishing she had brought a wrap with her. The August evening was not cold, but she shivered involuntarily on getting into the protection of the car.

She felt rather than saw Dominik's look towards her. Her mood was mellow in the extreme; she was relaxed and content, but disinclined to talk for the moment. As if he sensed this, he made no attempt at conversation. He turned on the radio and drove easily, relaxedly, fitting in with her mood and contributing to a comfortable silence by making no demands in any way.

It was not until they were almost back at the cottages that he spoke. 'I've enjoyed this evening, Diane, more than I can tell you. Thank you.'

'Thank you,' she said, meaning it but still not turning to look at him. She was looking out at the black nothingness of the country lanes around them, glancing up at the sky to see a perfect half-moon playing hide and seek with the clouds. She was aware of her situation, of her nearness to Dominik in the confines of the car . . . but she was trying not to think about that, about anything. She was, she knew, not as sober as she might be. The wine she had consumed had somehow taken the edges off reality and she was just . . . just being, just flowing with the now and what was happening. It was only when Dominik suggested she have a nightcap with him that she became alerted. 'A nightcap? Oh, I really think I've had enough to drink.'

'Which is very selfish of you,' he protested, 'given that I've had to abstain for the most part. Come on, Diane, have a goodnight drink with me.'

They were almost home. Home, at the cottages. She glanced at him, thinking it unfortunate that at the moment she happened to do so they were passing through a tiny village which had the occasional streetlight. His silhouette, his profile, she saw in sharp relief momentarily, but she could not see what was in his eyes because they were fixed firmly on the road. It did not, though, weaken her resolve. That she had been inviting trouble all evening, from the moment she had put this dress on, was something she was still aware of, in spite of the wine she had drunk. 'No, I'm going to pass on the nightcap, Nik. Thanks all the same.'

Suddenly the car was slowing, rapidly. It came to a halt and the engine was switched off, not angrily but certainly with a quick, decisive action on Nik's part. 'OK,' he said, with an irritation which was suppressed but discernible, 'what is it with you? What game are you playing, exactly? I want to know.'

'Game? I don't know what you mean . . .'

He just looked at her in the stillness, he looked hard and long and then, as if he had made a decision she would never be privy to, he switched the engine on again and pulled away. He accelerated, and they were turning into the cul-de-sac where the cottages were before Diane had time to sort out what had just happened.

All the lights in Rose Cottage were ablaze and they should not have been, not the upstairs lights, anyway. Diane knew something was wrong and she didn't think about following Dominik inside. Penny was barking, Nik was dashing upstairs—and Diane stood hesitantly at the foot of them, upset by the sound of Kirsty sobbing. A moment later she was dashing up the stairs herself, wondering why she had hesitated in the first place.

Mrs Archer was doing her best, she was shaking Kirsty by the shoulder, talking to her and attempting to reassure her, but to no avail. Kirsty was both awake and asleep at the same time, or so it seemed. Diane saw Dominik's look at

Mrs Archer, Mrs Archer's look of relief, and then her withdrawal from the scene. She saw Dominik gathering the child into his arms and crooning to her. His hand reached for the back of her head and he held her against him, talking, talking, talking.

'Kirsty, Kirsty . . . it's all right, baby. Uncle Nik is here and everything is all right. It's just a dream, that's all. It's all right. You're safe. You're safe, darling, and Uncle Nik is here . . .'

To Diane everything became blurred; she found herself blinking back tears. She was aware of Mrs Archer, aware of her anxiety, aware of herself and of what she was witnessing, and yet it was all suddenly unreal somehow. It took an effort for her to pull herself together, to make a contribution. She turned to the babysitter with a smile, telling her that everything would be all right now, that they should both go downstairs.

Whether it was ten, twenty or even thirty minutes before Nik came down, Diane didn't know. She had by then sent Mrs Archer home, reassuring her that Kirsty would be fine. The woman had looked at her gratefully and said that Mr Channing had warned her of this possibility. 'He said his niece had nightmares from time to time but—dear me, the poor child woke up screaming and I really didn't know what it was all about.'

'Diane? Has Mrs Archer gone?'

'Yes, she's gone home, Nik. Don't worry, she's fine; she was perturbed because she didn't understand—anyway, I told her. About Kirsty's mother, I mean. I hope you don't mind that? I thought it was only fair to explain.'

He waved a hand, looking weary suddenly, tired and . . . and defeated.

'Nik——' Diane could not finish the sentence for a

moment because she was choked, too emotional to speak. She had to shake herself, make another determined effort at composure. 'Let me get you a drink.'

He nodded, lowering himself into a chair and loosening his tie. Diane poured him a generous Scotch, shaking her head when he asked whether she was sure his taking Kirsty to a child psychologist was not a good idea. 'I didn't say that, Nik. I said I thought it unnecessary. The best thing we can do is—I mean the best thing you can do is to try to get her to talk about her mother. That's my opinion, for what it's worth. I think her talking about Jane, and about how she feels, will help her to come to terms with the situation.'

She found him smiling when she turned to face him; she put his drink on the table near his armchair, gasping when his hand closed tightly around her wrist. 'Come here.'

'Dominik——'

'I said come here.' He gave her no option, but tightened his grip and pulled her on to his lap, laughing when she landed inelegantly. The movement dislodged her dress, allowing more exposure of her breasts, not that she noticed. There was no opportunity to notice because Nik's arms closed around her and in one continuous movement he was kissing her.

Her resolve melted, and all the shoulds and should nots became irrelevant under the onslaught of his mouth. Again she was kissing him back, giving freely of herself and revelling in it. When his lips moved to kiss her cheeks, to nibble at her earlobes before trailing down along the side of her neck, she did not protest. When his lips came back to hers she responded hungrily, and when his hand closed gently around her breast she knew only how good it felt, how right it felt.

'How I want you!' He spoke against her lips, his mouth

refusing to break this contact with her. Then he was kissing her more deeply than ever, kissing her and shifting her slightly so she was lying across him, her upper body supported by his arm. Still there was no protest from her, there was no time to think, no time for anything except this willing, spontaneous reaction to him.

If she had felt her body yearning towards him earlier, it was nothing to the way she felt now; everything in her was crying out for more. She slid an arm around his neck to urge him closer, and when his lips moved away from hers she felt bereft. A second later she was gasping at the touch of his mouth against her breast, exposed fully to him by the smallest movement and cupped in his hand, its peak tautening even further as Dominik's lips closed over it. Gently to begin with, and then with a near roughness she felt she could never have enough of, he sucked and nipped at her, and all she could do was encourage him. The fingers of her right hand were pushed deeply into the crispness of his hair, firm against the back of his head, and beyond her closed eyes there was not a thought in her mind, there was nothing but Dominik and this, this gnawing, aching, longing for more.

'Diane——' Even as her eyes came open she was reaching for his hand, willing it back to her breast. 'All right, darling, but we'll have to move . . . this is impossible.' He eased her away from him, helping her to stand, and it was only then, foolishly, that she realised the extent of his arousal. In a voice which hardly sounded like his own, he said something about moving to the settee.

Had Kirsty not chosen that moment to shout down to him, Diane had no way of knowing what would have happened. In the few moments she had been separated from the touch of him, the feel of him, her mind had started to function—enough, at least, for her to realise how far things had gone. Even so, it took two more shouts from Kirsty before either she or Dominik could make a move, because for seconds they just looked at one another in disbelief.

'Heavens, she certainly picks her moments!' He turned to head for the door, stopping abruptly to look back at Diane with a humourless smile. 'I can't go up there, Diane. I need a moment . . . you go and see what she wants, would you?'

Wordlessly she complied, straightening her clothes into place before climbing the stairs. At the top of them there was a mirror in which she caught sight of herself. 'All right, Kirsty, I'll be with you in a jiff.'

'I only want a glass of water. What are you doing, Diane?'

She was combing her hair into place with her fingers. Outwardly she was trembling, inwardly she was actually shaking. What—how had it happened? How had it happened so quickly, so—and what the devil had she been thinking about? How could she have behaved so eagerly, so *wantonly?* Did she not know herself any more? Could that happen to a person? Apparently it could, because her reaction to Nik just now was something she would not have believed possible. Nor could she put it down to the wine she had drunk, because she was sober now and then some. Her mind was working overtime and there was nothing unclear about her thoughts at this moment.

'Diane?'

'I'm coming, poppet. I—my shoe just came off, that's all.'

Kirsty's room was lit only by a night-light. Diane was grateful for that, although she did not hesitate to move close to the child, to sit on the bed and take her hand. 'More bad dreams?'

'No. I haven't been back to sleep yet. I'm thirsty.'

'You're Kirsty?'

There was laughter from Kirsty, but all Diane could manage was a smile. That was how it had all begun with her and Nik's niece, and it was only a week ago. A week ago, and yet she felt she had known him a very long time.

'Any problems?' His voice came up the stairs, sounding normal again. 'Diane?'

'No, Nik. Don't bother coming up.' Diane's mind was racing, she was thinking how best to get out of this situation, out of the cottage, with the minimum of fuss. 'Listen, Kirsty, I'm going to say goodnight to you now, I'll send Uncle Nik up with a glass of water and I'll see you in the morning. OK? Will you come and have a cup of tea with me, and a little talk?'

'Course I will. What about? I mean what are we going to talk about?'

'Anything.' Diane shrugged, forgiving herself for this white lie. She knew exactly what form her talk with Kirsty would take, and she could only hope it would help the child.

Dominik was not pleased when she went down and announced she was going home; he didn't seem to understand what she was saying at first.

'I mean next door,' she said, avoiding his eyes. 'What did you think I meant?'

'I don't know what I thought. Diane——' When she side-stepped him, he moved quickly to catch hold of her, having to restrain himself from shaking her. 'You can't do this to me, Diane. Look at me——'

She could not, she was too embarrassed. 'I'm not doing anything to you, I'm just going home.'

'You know damn well what I mean. I said *look* at me!'

She looked at him, almost welcoming the anger that shot through her. 'I don't care for your tone, Dominik. Why don't you say what you're really thinking?' She lifted her chin, challenging him to be as honest with her as he liked her to be with him.

He was, to the point where she regretted her challenge. In no uncertain terms he told her what he was thinking—and what he was feeling. 'I want to make love to you and you're running away. You want me as much as I want you, but you're running away and I want to know *why*! Have you——'

'Nik, you're hurting my wrist. Let go of me, please.'

'Have you any idea how it feels to a man when——' He broke off, slackening his grip but keeping hold of her. The expression in his eyes softened and he shook his head slowly. 'Diane, I'm aching for you, don't you understand?'

She managed to nod, letting her eyes slide away from his; she did not want to see what was in them any more. 'I know.' It was a whisper, and it came hoarsely because there was the threat of tears behind her eyes. 'And yes, I do know how it feels.'

'Uncle Nik? Where's my water?'

He let go of Diane and she turned away, heading for the front door in what she hoped was a graceful exit.

CHAPTER SIX

'DIANE?'

'I'm in the living-room. Come in.'

Dominik followed the sound of her voice and found her sitting by the window, not turning to look at him. She was dipping her hand into a huge bag of peanuts and chomping on them as if it were somehow an act of defiance. The fingers of her free hand were strumming against her thigh and she still had not turned to look at him. It struck him as funny, seeing her so obviously uptight like that, and it was all he could do not to laugh out loud.

But he didn't, he just stood, looking at her profile against the brilliant sunlight streaming in through the window. For a few seconds he watched the play of light on her hair, blue-black and gloriously shiny. He wanted to go over and take her in his arms, to hold her, just hold her. In the bright yellow tracksuit she was wearing she looked far from sexy, but she did look . . . well, if he were just to hold her, to cuddle her against him, it wouldn't last long in any case. If he touched her at all he wanted her sexually, that much he knew from experience. Aloud he said, 'What am I going to do about you, Diane? And don't, please don't ask me what I'm talking about.'

With some reluctance she turned, glancing at him only briefly before turning her attention back to the bag of peanuts. Why had she bought them? They were very fattening and she had eaten almost all of them. It was out of character, too, for her to gorge herself like that. She had bought the peanuts when she had bought some milk and the Sunday papers earlier—not that she had looked at the papers, she had done nothing at all except think about Dominik. All the time she had been talking to Kirsty, she had been thinking about him.

'Good morning.' She didn't know what else to say. Yes, she knew what he was talking about but she didn't have the answer. What was he going to do about her? More to the point, what was she going to do about him? If only she weren't so uncertain of him, if only she were not convinced that as far as he was concerned this relationship of theirs was nothing more than—than a holiday romance. He had made no mention of seeing her once they went their separate ways, no mention of their meeting in London, perhaps, no mention of their meeting anywhere . . . So what did he want of her, expect of her? A casual fling? A very brief affair, hardly more than a one-night stand?

Well, that was not for her. No matter how much she wanted him, it was not for her. It wasn't her style, not the way she lived her life, to be made love to and then forgotten, as Eve had been forgotten by him, to the point where he regarded her as not existing any more. Or did he, really? Of course he didn't. Couldn't this be the reason he had made not even a hint of seeing her, Diane, at some point in the future? Geographically it would be so easy; he knew she was frequently in London and in any case she only lived in Maidstone. There were no excuses, there was only the reality of Eve and the reality of his feeling nothing more than a physical attraction for his temporary next-door neighbour.

'Diane, I asked you a question.'

She looked up to find him sitting, facing her, watching her speculatively. 'I—don't know what you're going to do,

Nik.'

'No, not that.' He smiled. 'I'd moved on from there, it was a rhetorical question anyway. I just asked you how things went with Kirsty.'

Kirsty. It was for her sake alone that Diane was staying at the cottage. Had it not been for the promise she had made to be with the child on her birthday, she would have packed up and gone back to Maidstone today. As it was, she had told Kirsty only a few minutes earlier that she would be leaving on Thursday morning, the day after her birthday.

'It went rather well, actually.' She was about to go on but he held up a hand, saying he would make them a cup of coffee first. 'I want to hear this verbatim,' he added, heading for the kitchen.

Diane let him get on with it. She had succeeded in getting Kirsty, not to talk about her mother, but at least to mention her more than once. The girl had also confessed that, while she was really looking forward to boarding-school, she was afraid in case the bad dreams continued and she would feel stupid in front of the other girls.

All of this was reported to Dominik when he came back with two mugs of coffee. 'So that's the top and bottom of it, Nik. That, and it seems the dreams are always about her being at her mother's funeral, as if she's reliving it.'

That news angered him; he pushed himself to his feet and stood with his back to Diane for a moment. 'I *knew* it was a mistake to let her go! It was Philip's idea. He insisted it was a good thing, that she was old enough to handle it, but I——'

'Well, he is her father.'

'Exactly! So what the hell could I do? And Kirsty wanted to be there—which didn't help my argument with Philip.'

They talked things over for a while, concluding that some

progress had been made, however small. At least Kirsty had begun to open up. 'What's she doing now?' Diane asked.

'She's sprawled on the floor with Penny, watching television.' He looked at his watch. 'It's getting on for twelve and we're wasting a gorgeous day. How about a bit of lunch and then an afternoon on the beach?'

'No, thanks.' Diane had been prepared for this and she was going to stick to her guns this time.

'Hey!' He came over to her, cajoling, taking both her hands in his. 'What is this? Are you angry with me?'

'For what?' She wanted not to look at him, she was not going to be persuaded . . . and if she looked into those warm brown eyes she might be.

'Had you said yes, that's the question I would have asked you. I've told you before,' he added, raising a hand to his lips, 'that I'll never apologise for wanting you.'

It was not the back of her hand he kissed this time; he turned her palm to his mouth and kissed her there, very provocatively, letting her feel the tip of his tongue against her skin. It was quite deliberate and she knew it, yet the sheer suggestion in it, the intimacy of it, succeeded in getting to her. To her chagrin she heard the sound of her breath catching in her throat and she pulled her hand away rapidly. 'Stop that!'

He merely laughed, looking at her with all the wickedness he was capable of. 'Come to the beach.'

'No.'

'But it's a beautiful day, my lovely. It's really hot, and I mean hot. Come on, come and play and swim and talk——'

'I said no.' She was weakening, she could feel it happening to her as if it were a physical process.

'But, Diane, I'll buy you ice-creams regularly, every hour on the hour.'

She had to bite her cheeks, she didn't dare to speak, so she just shook her head this time.

Dominik stood firm, looking down at her, crossing his arms over his chest with finality. 'And they will be *any flavour you want!*'

An hour later, when they were all on the beach, she reminded him of this promise and demanded a vanilla cornet at once. As soon as he left her to fetch said ice-cream, together with a chocolate one for Kirsty, Diane burst out laughing again. Well, maybe she was weak, but he could always make her laugh and she really liked that about him.

That evening, however, she did not invite further problems; she took her leave of Nik and Kirsty before they had dinner, saying truthfully that she wasn't hungry herself.

'It's all that ice-cream,' Nik said, reluctantly letting her out of the car outside Eden Cottage. 'It's spoiled your appetite.'

'Something like that.' Diane spoke lightly but she wasn't feeling light; in truth she had a headache, one that had been lingering all afternoon. Perhaps it had been a mistake to sit on the beach without a sun-hat today. Her pale skin was no longer pale, she had acquired a light tan by now, but she felt she'd had too much sun in any case. The August afternoon must have been something of a record-breaker for England.

After a long and fairly cool bath she felt better, enough to consider eating something, if only a sandwich. The question was, should she bother to get dressed again? It was almost nine o'clock by the time she finished blow-drying her hair, sitting at the dressing-table in just a bath towel.

Her eyes moved towards the wall connecting the two cottages and her decision was made; she would dress because she would not put it past Dominik to call on some pretext or other, once he'd put Kirsty to bed.

Which was exactly what he did. Within the hour he was knocking at the back door and Diane was moving quickly to unlock it. 'I saw your light was still on,' he was saying, grinning, 'so I knew you hadn't gone to bed yet.'

'You're not coming in, Dominik.' Diane blocked his path, fully prepared to fight him away if necessary.

'I'm not? Oh.' Taken aback but compliant, he shrugged his broad shoulders and smiled at her. He had changed into close-fitting trousers and a cotton T-shirt, as coal-black as his hair—hair which was still damp from the shower. Diane steeled herself, knowing it wasn't going to be so easy to get rid of him. Not that she wanted to, really, it was just . . . that she didn't want to be alone with him. He looked impossibly attractive. His T-shirt fitted like a second skin, and obscured nothing of the broad and muscular physique beneath it. Whatever he had used in the shower, his soap or whatever, was also catching her attention in the nicest way.

Inwardly cursing the effect he had on her, she stood firm this time. '*No*, Nik. Besides, you shouldn't leave Kirsty alone.'

He looked offended, exaggeratedly so. 'I haven't. Well, only for a minute. You may not believe this, but I came to borrow some milk, I really did.'

She did believe it; at least, she believed he needed some milk. Her own supplies were low but she had picked up a litre of milk that morning, together with the peanuts and newspapers. 'I'll buy that,' she told him, smiling finally. 'I've seen how bare you keep your cupboards. Right, I shall get the milk—and you will stay *right there*.' She stabbed a finger towards the step on which he was standing, but the moment she moved back into the kitchen he followed her.

'You——'

'Now, now, Diane, we don't want any name-calling. I need your advice.'

Her eyes narrowed. She was leaning against the sink unit, he was leaning against the kitchen table. It was a safe distance, and he really did seem to be serious; there was no amusement in his eyes. 'About what?'

'I . . . it's . . . well, it's Kirsty and her never-ending questions.'

'What now?'

He looked perplexed. 'She asks some very awkward ones, you see.'

'I know. So what's the latest? Do go on, Nik, it can't have been that awkward!'

From the look on his face, it had been. He was shrugging helplessly now. 'When I went to tuck her in tonight, she asked me about periods.'

Diane couldn't help herself, a short burst of laughter came out and she was grinning from ear to ear. 'So what did you tell her?'

'I didn't know what the hell to tell her! I—how could I?'

'But what's your problem? She's eleven years old, for heaven's sake, why not tell her the truth?'

'The truth? But—because she *is* only eleven, almost.'

'And this,' Diane said, unable to stop grinning, 'is the twenty-first century, almost. I know Kirsty's young for her years, but still. Besides, she must have had some information on the subject already, otherwise she wouldn't have used the right word.' Her advice, she thought, was sound; this was not something Nik was unable to handle, and she could not see his problem.

Unfortunately it was she who had the problem a moment later, when Nik went on, 'Well, actually, the way she

FREE BOOKS!

FREE GIFTS!

PLAY THE "LUCKY 7" SLOT MACHINE GAME !

AND YOU COULD GET FREE BOOKS, A FREE GOLD-PLATED CHAIN AND A SURPRISE GIFT!

NO COST! NO OBLIGATION TO BUY! NO PURCHASE NECESSARY!

PLAY "LUCKY 7" AND GET AS MANY AS SIX FREE GIFTS . . .

HOW TO PLAY:

1. With a coin, carefully scratch off the silver box at the right. This makes you eligible to receive one or more free books, and possibly other gifts, depending on what is revealed beneath the scratch-off area.

2. You'll receive brand-new Harlequin Romance® novels. When you return this card, we'll send you the books and gifts you qualify for *absolutely free!*

3. If we don't hear from you, every month we'll send you 8 additional novels to read and enjoy. You can return them and owe nothing but if you decide to keep them, you'll pay only $2.24* per book, a savings of 26¢* each off the cover price! There is *no* extra charge for postage and handling. There are no hidden extras.

4. When you join the Harlequin Reader Service®, you'll get our monthly newsletter, as well as additional free gifts from time to time just for being a member.

5. You must be completely satisfied. You may cancel at any time simply by sending us a note or a shipping statement marked "cancel" or returning any unopened shipment to us at our cost.

*Terms and prices subject to change without notice.
  Sales tax applicable in NY and Iowa.
© 1989 HARLEQUIN ENTERPRISES LTD.

You'll love your elegant 20k gold electroplated chain! The necklace is finely crafted with 160 double-soldered links and is electroplate finished in genuine 20k gold. And it's yours free as added thanks for giving our Reader Service a try!

DETACH AND MAIL CARD TODAY

PLAY "LUCKY 7"

Just scratch off the silver box with a coin.
Then check below to see which gifts you get.

YES! I have scratched off the silver box. Please send me all the gifts for which I qualify. I understand I am under no obligation to purchase any books, as explained on the opposite page.

(U-H-R-04/90)
118CIH FAV4

NAME

ADDRESS — APT

CITY — STATE — ZIP

7	7	7	WORTH FOUR FREE BOOKS, FREE GOLD ELECTROPLATED CHAIN AND MYSTERY BONUS
🍒	🍒	🍒	WORTH FOUR FREE BOOKS AND MYSTERY BONUS
●	●	●	WORTH FOUR FREE BOOKS
🔔	🔔	🍒	WORTH TWO FREE BOOKS

Offer limited to one per household and not valid to current Harlequin Romance subscribers.
All orders subject to approval. Terms and prices subject to change without notice.
© 1989 HARLEQUIN ENTERPRISES LTD.
PRINTED IN U.S.A.

HARLEQUIN "NO RISK" GUARANTEE
- You're not required to buy a single book—ever!
- You must be completely satisfied or you may cancel at any time simply by sending us a note or a shipping statement marked "cancel" or by returning any unopened shipment to us at our cost. Either way, you will receive no more books; you'll have no further obligation.
- The free books and gifts you receive from this "Lucky 7" offer remain yours to keep no matter what you decide.

If offer card is missing, write to:
Harlequin Reader Service, 901 Fuhrmann Blvd., P.O. Box 1867, Buffalo, N.Y. 14269-1867

DETACH AND MAIL CARD TODAY

BUSINESS REPLY CARD

First Class   Permit No. 717   Buffalo, NY

Postage will be paid by addressee

Harlequin Reader Service®
901 Fuhrmann Blvd.,
P.O. Box 1867
Buffalo, NY 14240-9952

NO POSTAGE
NECESSARY
IF MAILED
IN THE
UNITED STATES

worded it was a bit off-putting. What she actually wanted to know was why you wouldn't go for a swim today. She asked me whether you had your period.'

It was too much, too much because he was laughing now, not openly but with his eyes. At her. And she was blushing frantically; it had to be the worst blush of her entire life. Not knowing what else to do when Nik's laughter became audible, she turned her back on him and yanked open the refrigerator door.

'So what's your problem?' he asked, echoing her own words, and with the same nonchalance.

'I'll share this litre of milk with you.'

'Now you are furious, aren't you?'

'I'll have to find something to put it in.'

'Answer me.'

'Go to hell, Dominik.'

'Very nice!' He roared with laughter. '*Now* who's embarrassed?'

'I am not embarrassed.' She turned to glare at him. 'Here, take it all, I have enough for the morning until I go shopping.'

'Talk to me, woman.'

'Talk to you? *Talk* to you! I think I hate you!'

Dominik stepped closer, privately delighted by the loveliness of her flushed face and her wild green eyes. Her hair flew silkily backwards as her head snapped up, eyes outraged, telling him to keep his distance. But he would never keep his distance from this girl, not if he could help it.

That thought pulled him up abruptly; he froze for a second, recognising the symptoms. He had felt this way before and it hadn't been real. It wasn't real now, either, he knew that deep inside. It was just the obvious attraction.

To Diane's relief, he did keep his distance; she had no idea what had just gone through his mind, but he sobered visibly. 'Your milk,' she said, thrusting the carton at him.

'Thanks.' He nodded, looked at her strangely and added, 'You said you were going shopping tomorrow morning?'

'Yes. Did you want me to get you something?' Calmer now, she found herself in a position to tease. 'Like milk and sugar and bread and eggs and——'

'All right, all right. Honestly, anyone would think I neglected to feed Kirsty!'

'I'm only glad to know you have a housekeeper,' Diane retorted, 'otherwise, I really might begin to worry.'

'About what?'

'About Kirsty always eating in restaurants. It's no substitute for home cooking. Which reminds me, I'd thought of making the meal myself on Wednesday, for her birthday.'

'No.' The word came firmly. 'I want you to enjoy yourself, I don't want you slaving over a hot stove.'

'I could make a salad——'

'*No.* Besides, it's all arranged, a surprise birthday cake and all. We're going to Rakes, in Fordingbridge.'

'Rakes? Is that supposed to mean something to me?'

'No, though it's been there for some years. It's owned these days by two men who are not only charming and obliging, they also know what they're doing. So we shall have the birthday dinner there and let the restaurant worry about the washing-up, all right?'

'Would there be any point in arguing with you?'

'None at all.'

'Then why ask if it's all right?'

'Because,' he said, moving closer, his eyes glinting with a look she knew only too well, 'I'm loath to finish this conversation, loath to go back next door and leave you all alone.'

It provoked more of a giggle than a laugh from her. 'You mean *you* don't want to be alone.'

'I have Beethoven for company.'

'And I have a good book.'

'But it's not the same, is it, Diane?' She would have answered that had he given her the chance, but he was walking away from her and she found herself looking at his back.

'Goodnight, Nik.'

'About tomorrow. You'll be free after you've done your shopping?'

'No. Don't look at me like that. You can argue till you're blue in the face this time, and you can promise me all the ice-creams under the sun, but this time, I win. I want to have a rest tomorrow. I feel I need it.'

His initial reaction was puzzlement, then he looked at her as if trying to gauge whether she was serious. 'You're not feeling ill, are you? Tell me honestly, darling . . .'

They both heard the word, the endearment, the moment it was spoken. Neither reacted in even the smallest way but it had come as a surprise to them both.

'Diane?'

'Not at all. Let's leave it till Tuesday, Nik.'

He left her then, putting up no further argument, and although she expected to see him on her doorstep at some point the next day he did not turn up. Neither did Kirsty, who had obviously been warned off by her uncle.

The result of this for Diane was a feeling of disappointment so acute that it should have made her realise what was happening to her. It didn't, she tried not to think about it at all, acknowledging only that Dominik had got under her skin to the point where she missed him after merely a one-day absence.

Tuesday and Wednesday were very different. They were days full of laughter and, miraculously, more unbroken sunshine. The birthday dinner at Rakes was an all-round success; they all ate too much, but only the adults regretted it.

When they got back to the cottage it was to be greeted by a Great Dane who barked and leapt about so enthusiastically that what was left of Kirsty's birthday cake very nearly ended up on the carpet. A generous slice ended up on the floor in any case, on a plate for Penny at Kirsty's insistence.

It was more than an hour later before silence reigned at last. Diane and Nik looked at one another from the comfort of their respective armchairs and sighed in unison. He looked at his watch. 'Right, it sounds as if she's finished her dallying in the bathroom. I'll just go up and kiss her goodnight . . . you're not going to run out on me, are you?'

Diane looked up at him as he stood, smiling and shaking her head. No, she wasn't going to run out on him tonight, not on this, her last night. She was leaving in the morning and—and that would be it. He still had made no mention of seeing her after she got back to Maidstone. 'No, not tonight. I'll stay and have a farewell drink with you, Nik.'

It was not until he came down again that she got a response. He clearly had not registered that she was going home. 'What did you mean, a farewell drink?'

Diane shrugged. 'Just that. You know I'm leaving here tomorrow——'

'No, I *don't* know that.' He was staring at her, obviously annoyed. 'I mean I didn't know that. Why didn't you mention this?'

'But I did——'

'Not to me, you didn't.'

'Oh. Well, I told Kirsty and that's as good as telling you directly, isn't it?'

'No, it isn't. Not this time it isn't. I knew nothing about this.'

It was difficult to conceal her pleasure at his reaction—but she was misunderstood. He was still annoyed. 'I don't think this is something to smile about, Diane. I think you should have *told* me. *Me.*'

'Well, I—I'm sorry.'

'And what are you leaving for? What's the hurry? You booked the cottage for two full weeks.'

'Which doesn't mean I'm bound to stay the full time. I have things to do, Nik. The completion on my new flat takes place next week and——'

Again he cut her off. He was standing in the middle of the room, looking at her as if she were mad. 'You didn't tell me that, either. What is it with you? What day next week?'

'On Wednesday,' she said lamely, wondering why it mattered.

'Wednesday. So when will you move in?'

'The same day. Wednesday afternoon.'

He paused, shaking his head at her. 'OK, give me your telephone number.'

'At the flat?' She managed to suppress her smile, not wishing to irritate him further.

'Of course at the flat.'

'I haven't got a phone number yet.'

'Then give me your father's phone number.' He took a pad and pencil from a small desk in the corner and handed it to her. When she gave it back, having written her father's telephone number on it, he gave her a white business card.

'This has all my telephone numbers on it,' he said,

putting the pad back on the desk. 'So if I don't reach you before Wednesday, you ring me, OK? I want to see you again, Diane, just as often as I can. This is no farewell drink we're having.'

At that point, he went over to the cupboard and began to pour drinks for them both. 'So what exactly is the hurry? Why leave tomorrow? It's only Thursday.'

'I have things to do, I told you. I've got a lot of belongings at home, I mean at my father's, and they have to be packed.'

'Why can't you do that on Sunday? You're not shifting furniture, are you?'

'No, but my father comes back from his honeymoon on Sunday and——'

'His *honeymoon*?'

It was Diane's turn to stare. What had she said now? 'I did tell you my father had remarried, I distinctly remember telling you he'd recently——'

'Yes, you did. But you did not mention that it was *so* recent. Will you never cease to amaze me, woman? What—I'm beginning to think I don't understand you at all. Why didn't you tell me your father was on his honeymoon?'

She was at a loss. 'I didn't think it relevant.'

'Listen to me, Diane. Firstly I think there's more to it than that, secondly it is relevant. It's relevant because you omitted——' He broke off, both frustrated and irritated. He took a long, slow breath and started again. 'Why are you so reluctant to tell me things about yourself? There is nothing about you and your life that is irrelevant to me. Why is it so difficult to open up to me? It's called communication, Diane. There's nothing complicated about it.'

'All right,' she said, lamenting his irritation with her even as she felt glad about it because it told her his interest was genuine. 'What would you like to know?'

'Everything.' He was smiling again, much to her relief. 'Let's see . . . what's your new stepmother like?'

She didn't think about her answer, she described her new stepmother graphically, determined to communicate, since that was what Nik wanted. 'A good question, Nik. Her name is Annabel, she's a blue-eyed blonde, one of those about whom you would say butter wouldn't melt. She's pretty and she knows it, and she's also a manipulator; she's cunning and devious and she thinks that I'm not aware of it. She's twenty years younger than my father, who's fifty-three, and she started exploiting him the moment they met.'

Diane was off and running, not noticing the way Dominik's brows had risen. He was walking towards her with her drink, which he placed, wordlessly, on the coffee-table next to the business card he had given her.

'This is the main reason I'm moving out of my father's bungalow, practicalities aside. I can't bear to watch Annabel using him any more. She has an eight-year-old son, Bobby, to whom my father has also become a meal ticket—though I've nothing whatever against the child, he's really sweet and——'

'Good grief!' Dominik cut in, bemused by her uncharacteristic vehemence. 'I think I can safely conclude that you don't like the woman!'

'Very safely.'

'Does your father know how you feel?'

'Of course he does. I told him before he married her, but he just can't see it, he thinks I'm quite wrong about Annabel.'

'Maybe you are.'

She looked sharply at him, shaking her head avidly. 'No. She's been wrapping my father around her little finger since the moment they met. He fell hook, line and sinker for her doll-face.'

'How did they meet?' Dominik suppressed a smile at the expression Diane had used; he had a few things to say to her, but he wanted to hear more first. 'Was it in a social setting?'

'No. At work. My father's an auditor and he met her when he was sent on an audit at the head office of Dunningham's the stationers. Annabel had just started there as a telephonist. I knew before he even brought her home to meet me what type she was.'

'Oh, come on, now! You knew nothing of the sort. What could you know, before you'd met her?'

Diane's eyes flashed angrily. He seemed to be missing the point, and it wasn't like him. 'The things my father told me, of course.'

'Like what?'

'Like the fact that she's twenty years younger.'

'What of it?'

She inclined her head in acknowledgement. 'OK, of itself that's by no means the end of the world. But you're missing the point. I've told you how pretty she is; she set out to make a catch of my father and she succeeded. He isn't a wealthy man, but he's clever with investments and that sort of thing, and he is comfortably off—he also has a ready-made home of his own. Now, Annabel has a son, she hated her job at Dunningham's and she's given up work altogether now. So draw your own conclusions, Dominik.'

His answer began with an expansive shrug. 'I'm not saying you're wrong, my lovely, but you might be. Do consider that. If Annabel is so pretty, finding herself a man, a husband, would surely present no problem—with or without her eight-year-old son. So why should she pick on your father? Couldn't she have gone after someone who *is* wealthy—and nearer her age? In other words, why are you taking it for granted that she doesn't genuinely love your father?'

'Because she loves herself, that's why.'

'You mean she's vain?'

'Well, no, not exactly.' Diane shifted in her chair, at a loss to understand why Nik seemed to be championing this woman he had not even met. It occurred to her that he might be winding her up deliberately, for reasons best known to himself, but her acknowledging this possibility did nothing to lessen her annoyance with him. 'Are you playing games with me, Dominik?'

The question amused him and he did nothing to hide it. He looked straight into her eyes as he answered. 'If there's anyone in this room who plays games, darling girl, it's you.'

'And what's that supposed to mean?'

His gaze didn't waver, didn't budge. 'You know very well what it means.'

Diane looked away, more uncomfortable than ever. It seemed safer to stick with the subject of Annabel, but there was really nothing more to say on that score. 'Anyway, let's leave the subject of my scheming stepmother; she's not my favourite topic of conversation.'

'You need to look at that,' she was told. 'It's not exactly a healthy attitude, is it? Couldn't you try to get on with her for your father's sake?'

'You think I haven't tried?' Diane's protest came loudly. 'Give me some credit, please! I've tried and tried, but I just can't get on with her. How can I, when I can see straight through her?'

'You might be blinded by your own bias, by your own assumptions that——'

'I hear what you're saying,' she cut in angrily, 'and I've

considered all that. It simply is not the case.'

'You're not giving her a chance, Diane, you——'

'Please, leave it alone! I don't want to discuss her any further.'

'Shut up and listen, Taurus! My goodness, you really are stubborn, aren't you?'

She shut up, taken aback by his tone; he wasn't teasing her, he was really irritated. Why? What difference did all this make to him? To him and her? To him and her . . . was there such a thing? He seemed determined to pick a fight. Why? Because this was her last night, because he didn't really want to see her again? He was talking but she hardly heard a word of it; she was looking at his card, lying on the table beside her, and wondering whether that had been nothing more than a polite gesture. Maybe he hadn't meant what he'd said about wanting to see her again. Well, she would not ring him, she would just have to wait and see whether he contacted her or whether this would prove to be nothing more than his tactful withdrawal from their relationship. He was a sensitive man; he might have given her his phone numbers and said his pretty words to make her feel better about leaving tomorrow. It was a sickening thought, but it was by no means impossible.

'Diane? Are you listening to me?'

'To every word,' she lied, feeling vaguely sick at a physical level now. What *was* the matter with her? It was only then that she heard the warning bells in her head, knowing as she did so that they had in fact been ringing for some time, for days . . . She was falling in love with Dominik Channing. Wasn't she?

'Diane? You look dismayed,' he said, looking puzzled himself. 'What's the matter?'

'I—nothing. Nothing at all.'

'You're lying,' he told her, smiling a gentle sort of smile. 'And you weren't listening, either.'

'You were saying something about Kirsty's father.'

Dominik looked heavenward. 'My dear girl, I was actually pointing out that your attitude towards Annabel is not unlike my attitude to Philip Nolan. But I've changed my attitude, thanks to you and the things you pointed out. That's what communication with people does, it helps put things into perspective, for one thing. I was grateful for your objectivity regarding Kirsty's father, so why won't you listen to what I'm saying about your stepmother?'

'Because this is different,' she snapped.

It didn't occur to her how stubborn she was being; it didn't occur to her that, had she heard his remarks at any other time, she would have reacted differently. Nor did she realise that she was missing Dominik's point entirely; she was too concerned with her own realisation of a minute earlier and the result of this was a new rush of anger. 'It's different, and you really don't know what you're talking about!'

He threw up his hands. 'OK. We'll leave it, then. Let me get you another drink.'

'No. I'm going.'

They were both standing; Diane was reaching for her bag and Dominik was closing in on her. His arms came around her and her bag slipped from her grasp. 'Like hell you're going.' He spoke and laughed softly, pulling her easily against the length of his body. 'At this hour? On our last night?'

She closed her eyes for fear he would see the emotion in them. On their last night? *Had* she been right, then, in thinking what she had thought earlier? Her mind went into overdrive and her foolish heart did the same thing, creating in her a feeling of resentment towards him which made no sense at a logical level. But logic was not in the scheme of things at the moment, not for her, and neither was honesty. 'To tell you the truth, I'm not feeling too good.'

'You feel very good to me.' He spoke against her ear, his face nuzzling against her hair. He could feel the rapid beat of her heart, his own heart, and the swift arousal the mere touch of her always provoked in him. 'Darling, please listen to me, I mean really listen this time. Haven't we reached the point where you can be honest with me *all* the time? I don't believe you're feeling unwell. When are you going to stop holding back? Supposing I tell you what you're really feeling . . .' His voice trailed off and his lips began to travel from her ear to her neck to the base of her throat, coming to rest at the tell-tale pulse beating there.

More warning bells started ringing. Diane stiffened and pushed her hands between their bodies, laying them flat against his chest. He didn't need to tell her what she was feeling, not at the physical level, that was obvious to them both. She was already breathless and well aware of the signals her body was sending to him. The difference was that her mind had other ideas. 'Dominik, let go of me.' She pushed against his chest as she spoke, but she knew it was ineffectual, that he had released her simply because he would not hold her by force. That was not the way he went about things.

'Diane——'

'No! I don't want to hear any more, I don't want to talk any more. Not now, not tonight. Now just let me go, please.'

Dominik was doing nothing to prevent her from doing just that, nor would he. He made the decision to leave her be reluctantly, trusting his instinct, if instinct was what it was. Whatever, something was telling him to comply with her wishes, and as a result of this he let her see herself out. For seconds he remained standing, still feeling her presence. But she had gone and he really had no idea why. It had been a strange evening. What had happened? Was it him or was it her? His eyes alighted on the card he had given to her, still lying on the coffee-table. And what did this mean? Had she forgotten it or had she ignored it? Why had she not put it into her bag when he had given it to her?

He looked around for his cigars, found them and lit one, his first of the day. He was aware of his eyes focusing as if of their own accord on the wall separating their cottages. How many times had they done that during these past ten days? Was that all it was, ten days? Ten days and she was really under his skin, he acknowledged that. He acknowledged also that there had been nothing different about his own behaviour, that it was indeed Diane who had been somehow different tonight; she had been in a strange mood. Well, women and their moods were by no means things with which he was unfamiliar.

He smiled into the silence and closed his eyes, planning to speak to her before she left in the morning, and to give her the card she had forgotten.

Next door, Diane was packing. She wanted to make an early start so she would have a clear day; in any case, it was not quite bedtime, so she might as well do something useful. Nor was she remotely tired; sleep would not come rushing to take her into oblivion tonight, regardless of the hour.

She smiled at that thought several hours later, when she was lying in the silence of her bedroom. Through the honey-coloured curtains the light of the moon was shining, the same moon she had watched from Dominik's car last

Saturday, driving back from Bournemouth. It was fuller now, very bright tonight.

He had, she thought, been in a strange mood this evening, and although she wondered why, she was determined not to start analysing. Not this time, not now. There was absolutely no point, and in any event she had realised that, even if she were not in love with him, then she was certainly in danger of it. So what could she do, really, but leave that in the hands of Fate? Either he would contact her again or he would not.

She could only hope he would.

At first light she woke, having slept fitfully and only briefly at that. Twenty-five minutes later she was driving away from the row of terraced cottages and their still-sleeping inhabitants.

CHAPTER SEVEN

'YOU went away?' Annabel was saying, making no effort to conceal her puzzlement. 'To Boscombe? But you never mentioned to us——'

'It was a last-minute decision.' Diane shrugged, looking from her stepmother to her father. The newlyweds had arrived home just an hour earlier, and were enjoying the second pot of tea Diane had made for them.

They had been talking about their time in Madrid, about the things they had seen, and she had listened with genuine interest. She had also made an effort to listen to Annabel with different ears, unbiased ears, and to try to give her the benefit of the doubt. Since leaving Eden Cottage the previous Thursday, the point Dominik had tried to make had finally penetrated; it was true that her attitude towards Annabel was not unlike Dominik's attitude towards Philip Nolan. So it was not only for her father's sake that she was making a real effort now, it was for Annabel's sake and equally for her own.

'That isn't like you, love. Last-minute decisions, I mean.' This came from her father, and Diane smiled at him, feeling happy because *he* was so obviously happy . . . and hoping that it really would, could, last.

'I know. I normally plan ahead, don't I? Well, I had a few things to think over, so I took off.'

'Like what?' her father asked. 'And why bother going away when you had the bungalow to yourself?'

'Perhaps she felt like a change of scene, Frank.' Annabel

drained her cup and refilled it, but not before offering more tea to her husband and Diane first.

Diane declined. 'No, not for me, thanks. I want to press on, there are books to be packed—though I think that's about it.'

'You've packed everything else? Well, let me help you with your books, at least.'

Diane looked at her stepmother and tried to read what was in her eyes. Was this offer of help made because Frank was listening, because she couldn't wait to see the back of his daughter—or for a much simpler reason? 'Thanks, but no. You have all your unpacking to do and you must be tired from your journey. Excuse me, I'll see you later.'

Well, it was a start. Dominik would approve. Dominik. As she packed her not inconsiderable store of books, Diane thought about him constantly. It was nothing new, she had hardly stopped thinking about him since Thursday morning. No, more accurately, she had hardly stopped thinking about him since the day she had met him. She had hardly left the bungalow, too, since getting back—but he hadn't phoned her.

She supposed he was still at Rose Cottage, until today, at least; she had understood that he would be there until Sunday. Then back to his house in London, with a disgruntled Kirsty, no doubt.

Thinking about Kirsty made her think about Bobby, Annabel's son. Annabel was not going to collect him from his father in Scotland until Wednesday, which was just as well. What would now be Bobby's bedroom alone was full of boxes, cartons of Diane's belongings. Her father was taking a day off work on Wednesday and helping her move in a hired van. Her furniture should start to arrive on Wednesday afternoon, at the flat, at least in theory. This

was all new to her, ordering furniture and moving
and—being on her own. Living on her own. She wondered
how she would like it. That in the course of her travels she
spent many nights away alone in hotel rooms was no
indication of what it would be like actually living alone.

A week later, as she stood in the kitchen of her new flat
looking down at the road three storeys below, Diane
thought she would make the adjustment quite easily.
Although she had only been here since Wednesday, she had
not felt lonely . . . not if she discounted the awful yearning
to see Dominik again.

During the middle of the afternoon she made minor
adjustments to the placing of the furniture, which she had
juggled several times, both in her living-room and in her
dining-room. Everything had worked out beautifully; her
bedroom suite had been delivered as promised on the
Wednesday afternoon and everything else during Thursday
and Friday. Her father had given her a lump sum of money
towards her move away from home, and she had used it as a
deposit on the flat itself. She had wiped out her own savings
buying furniture for cash, and she was now one of the
millions of people who had a mortgage around their
necks—not that that worried her. After a three-week break
from work, she would be on the job again starting
tomorrow, and her busiest season was ahead of her. If it
proved to be a really good season, she might just go abroad
at the end of January or early February when things
slackened off.

The telephone rang. It had been connected two days
earlier but no one other than her father had rung her here
yet.

'Idiot!' she chided herself as she went to answer it, wishing it would be Dominik. No one other than her father *had* her new telephone number as yet!

It was Annabel, sounding anxious and vaguely embarrassed. 'Diane, it's Annabel. I—your father's out fishing with Bobby so I wasn't sure what to do. I mean, what to say.'

'About what?'

'Sorry, yes, I'm not making sense. Well, I've just had a telephone call from someone called Dominik Channing. He knew my name and he wanted to know if you were on the phone yet; he wanted me to give him the number.'

Diane closed her eyes, wishing she could just shout out her pleasure at this news. 'And did you?' she asked, too quickly, too eagerly. 'Did you give it to him, Annabel?'

There was a momentary silence. 'No—but I can see I should have. Look, Diane, please understand, I didn't want to do anything without consulting you first. He said it would be all right with you, but how was I to know that? He said he'd met you when you were in Boscombe, that he was living in the cottage next door to you but——'

'All of which is true.'

'Oh. I—you made no mention of him to me or your father.'

'I'm aware of that.' Quickly, Diane added, 'But not to worry, if he's really keen he'll ring you back, won't he?'

Her stepmother's relief was palpable; she had obviously expected more unpleasantness between them. 'That's right. But I did offer to ring him back myself. I said I'd check with you first and if you wanted him to have your number, I'd ring him back.'

It was only then that Diane realised how tightly she was holding the receiver. 'And what did he say?'

'He told me not to bother.'

Diane's eyes closed, her heart feeling suddenly like lead. *What* had he meant by that?

'Diane? I was saying, he didn't seem annoyed or anything. He just said he understood my reasons for not wanting to give him your number and—that I shouldn't bother ringing him back. He said a polite goodbye and hung up, didn't even give me his telephone number.'

'Look, it's OK. You did the right—well, you did what you thought was best. Forget it now, Annabel, because, as I said, if he does want to talk to me he will ring you back.'

Dominik never did ring Annabel back. Instead he turned up at Diane's new home in person. Her buzzer rang within an hour of her talking to her stepmother.

She invited him up in a voice as casual as she could possibly make it, released the security lock on the outside door and waited for the sound of the lift arriving on the third floor. It was all she could do to breathe normally while she waited; worrying about her appearance was pointless because she had no time to do anything about it.

'Well,' he said, the moment they were face to face, 'aren't you the naughty girl, not ringing me? Here, welcome to your new home.'

It was as if they had never been apart. He spoke to her with that wicked glint in his eyes, giving her a smile which was nothing short of devastating. In his hand was a beautiful arrangement of flowers made up in a basket, in oasis, which Diane accepted with a little squeal of pleasure. 'Thank you, Nik. They're gorgeous, just gorgeous!'

'You and they both,' he said, letting his eyes roam over every inch of her. 'You're looking good—and I've missed you. Well, come on, woman, aren't you going to invite me inside? Am I not welcome here?'

She stepped back, her free arm gesturing expansively

towards the living-room. 'Of course you're welcome.'

'There's no "of course" about it,' he said, glancing quickly at her as he preceded her inside. 'You left my business card in my cottage quite deliberately, and you haven't phoned me in over a week. I *am* in the telephone directory, so there was really no excuse.'

'I've been very busy.' She spoke without apology, placing the flowers lovingly on a coffee-table. 'You can see that for yourself now.'

He was looking around, nodding slowly and seeming impressed. 'Very nice, too. Show me the rest of it.'

He got a guided tour and, when it was over, the offer of coffee or tea. He settled for tea. 'Are you going to be happy here, Diane?'

'I think so. There's only one drawback, it being a third-floor flat. I like to bring my samples in and hang them up, but that's going to involve traipsing down in the lift with a garment rail. Still, it can be done. Apart from that, my only criticism is the colour of the carpet. I mean, it's a nice idea that lots of new buildings are sold carpeted these days—but this isn't what I would have chosen.' She wrinkled her nose, looking down at the petrol blue-green of the carpet uncertainly.

'I like it,' Dominik told her, smiling that gorgeous smile of his. 'It's neutral, it doesn't impinge. You could have put any style or colour of furniture in here without it clashing.'

'I suppose so.' Diane got up to make the tea, and he followed her and stood in the kitchen doorway, leaning negligently against the frame. 'Have you missed me?'

'I've had no time to miss anyone or anything.' She kept her back to him so he wouldn't see her grinning. Had she missed him? Oh, if only he knew!

'Well, life just hasn't been the same for me,' he went on,

but not without a smile in his voice. 'There's been no one to aggravate me, frustrate me, argue with me—except for Kirsty, of course.'

Diane glanced over her shoulder, frowning. 'How is she? Any more nightmares recently?'

'None at all, not since the night you were there. She seems a lot brighter and she's actually talked about her mother on two different occasions. She's even mentioned how much she's looking forward to seeing her father at Christmas, and I said nothing to dampen that enthusiasm. I just hope to goodness that Philip turns up as promised.'

'Christmas? He'll be back before the end of the year, then?'

'So he says. He phoned me a few days ago. I don't know how he's managing it, since his contract is supposed to be till the end of the year, but that's his business. He reckons to get back on the day before Christmas Eve.'

'That's great news, Dominik!'

He nodded, shrugging. 'I will give him his due, he said he wants to spend Christmas with his daughter. He'll be staying with me, of course, until he finds a place of his own. Happily, he isn't short of money.'

'Good. And I'm glad you're giving him his due; he sounds sincere enough to me. I'd like to meet him.' The words were out before she even thought about them. Christmas was a long way away; there was nothing to say she would still be seeing Dominik by then, nothing at all.

Yet he seemed to take it for granted. 'Of course you'll meet him. Kirsty has already mentioned the idea of having a party—in Philip's honour. If that comes off, you'll meet him then.'

Diane turned and handed him the tea-tray. 'Make yourself useful, I have to pop into the bathroom.'

She had to drag a comb through her hair, at least. Changing into something other than the jeans and sweatshirt she was wearing would be too obvious, but at least she could comb her hair and do something about the shine on her nose. All morning she had been cleaning, although the place had been immaculate before the furniture had started arriving. Virtually everything was done now, though, everything put away and spick and span. Very satisfying. Later this evening she would be tending to her samples, ironing any woollens which needed it, and planning her route for the coming week.

Dominik had other ideas. He wanted her to go back to London with him, to have dinner at his house. 'Kirsty's longing to see you again,' he added, making her wonder whether this invitation was for the child's benefit or for his own.

It was both. Dominik saw her hesitation and smiled, wishing she had opted to sit next to him on the settee rather than taking the armchair at a right-angle to him. It was typical of her to keep her distance, though, and he had stopped being surprised by it. What Diane was afraid of he still had no idea, but he did know that the attraction between them was making itself felt even across this distance, and beyond the conversation they were having, more strongly than ever before. It was just . . . *there*, existing independently.

Hell, he had missed her! He might have got up there and then, to cross over to her and take her into his arms, but she was shaking her head and saying there was no way she could have dinner with him tonight.

'Why?' The word came too strongly from him, too quickly and with too much of a hard edge. It surprised him as much as it did Diane, and the extent of his disappointment was a revelation to him.

Diane felt indignant; she didn't like the way he had demanded an explanation, and she did not like the implication that he had taken her for granted. That he had just materialised out of the blue was one thing—but what was he supposing? That her life had simply ground to a halt during this past week and a half, that she had had nothing else to do but sit and wait for him to come along and invite her out? 'I just can't at such short notice,' she said firmly. 'I have other plans.'

'A date?'

She looked at him quickly, seeing an impassive face, nothing telling in the beautiful dark brown eyes. 'No. For one thing, I'm going to my father's for dinner. I've been eating there most evenings, until I get myself organised.'

He smiled at this news. 'In spite of Annabel?'

'In spite of Annabel. She's . . . been very civil since she got back. And so have I.' She returned Dominik's smile and inclined her head, shrugging slightly. 'I'm making allowances, trying to bear in mind the point you made. In other words, I'm giving her a chance.'

'Good. I'd like to meet her some time. Her and your father, of course. And what was the other thing?'

Diane looked at him blankly, taken aback by his wanting to meet her father and her stepmother. 'The other thing? Oh, I see what you mean.' She went on to explain the rest of her plans for the evening. 'I have to get myself geared for work, I've been off for three weeks.'

'All right. So when can I see you? I and Kirsty. Do make an effort, Diane—I'm taking her down to Devon on Thursday week; she's starting at her new school, and she very much wants to see you before she leaves.'

'So soon? But of course, we're almost into September,

aren't we? Well, how about next weekend?'

'How about during the week?' he countered, smiling again. 'Like tomorrow, for instance?'

'Oh, Nik, I'm sorry but I just can't.' She was sorry, too, more than he could know, more than she would show. 'I'm going to be in Shropshire for the first part of the week,' she explained, going on to tell him that she would be away from the flat until Thursday. Her customers in that area were the farthest out in her territory, but they had to be seen just as regularly as the ones nearer home. 'And Thursday night won't suit me because I'll be shattered.'

'Friday, then?'

'Friday. Done.'

'And Saturday.'

'Saturday?'

'I have to go to a party,' he informed her, not looking particularly enthusiastic about it.

'Have to?'

'A business thing, sort of. Put it this way: if I don't turn up, a prospective customer will be offended.'

'Then turn up by all means,' Diane laughed. 'Am I to take it you need an escort?'

'Want, not need. Yes, I want you to come with me, Diane. And you can go to town, it'll be a very swish affair, in a private house. Formal dress.'

Go to town? Formal dress? The prospect was vaguely frightening, but she wasn't going to let Nik know that. Already she was wondering what she would wear.

He left around five, pausing by her front door just long enough to brush his lips lightly against hers. His smile was rueful. 'I don't want to go, but I have to. I told Kirsty I'd be back by six, with or without you.'

'You could have brought her here, Nik.'

He smiled but said nothing. He had not known how welcome he would be, not really; he still didn't know where he stood with this mysterious woman.

From his jacket he took another business card, which he placed very deliberately in her hand, closing her fingers around it. 'My home address is on there. Shall we say six o'clock on Friday? It has to be early because of Kirsty. If you'd like me to come and collect you, we'll make it——'

'There's no need for that.' She smiled at the idea; she knew the centre of London very well and driving in it did not daunt her. 'I'm more than capable of getting there under my own steam, Dominik.'

'I don't doubt it. You're capable of a lot of things, darling girl.' Half to himself, he grinned, letting the implication hang in the air so she could make of it what she might. 'I was thinking only about the hassle of parking.'

Parking did not present a problem, although that was admittedly something of a miracle, most particularly on a Friday evening.

The nights had started to darken earlier, but as yet it was far from being dark at six o'clock. A fine rain was falling when Diane got out of her car, the sort of rain which somehow managed to wet a person even more than a full-fledged shower. She hurried along the street with her head down, glancing only once at the number on a door until she stopped outside Dominik's number seventeen. There was a brass plate outside and it was only then that she realised his offices and his home were at one and the same place. Well, there was certainly no shortage of space. She climbed the five steps to the front door and rang the bell which had a tiny notice saying "Private Residence" beneath it. The other notice said 'Dominik Channing Properties', and it was Dominik who opened the door to her.

The house was huge, built at the turn of the century, probably, and one in a long terraced row, on four storeys plus attics.

'I hadn't realised your offices were here,' she said, smiling up at him as he took hold of her hand in welcome. 'I should have, since there was no separate address on your card, except for the one in Christchurch.'

'That's strictly for the rental side of my business,' he said, leading her to a staircase at the end of the long hallway. His offices occupied the whole of the ground floor, to their right, but he ignored them as if they didn't exist, though lights were shining in two of them, beyond the reeded glass doors.

Kirsty was standing at the top of the stairs with Penny, shifting impatiently from one foot to the other. 'Diane! Oh, I'm so glad to see you! He wouldn't let me come down with him, you know, to let you in. Wasn't that *mean*?'

Diane laughed, understanding Nik's reason when she found herself almost bowled over by the child's enthusiastic hug. 'Steady on, Kirsty! Anyone would think I hadn't seen you for a year!'

'It feels like a year. Why haven't you been here till now? And why didn't you telephone Uncle Nik? He hasn't been out with anyone else, you know, since he met you.'

'*That* is enough!' The words came from the man in question and, though they were not spoken without a little amusement, the warning in them was very strong. 'Give Diane a chance to catch her breath, child. And take her jacket for her. I'll show her the way to the living-room.'

Elegance! All around her there was elegance in the form of paintings and fine furniture, much of which was antique, much of which made Diane's eyes open in astonishment. Dominik's home was nothing, but nothing, like she had expected it to be. Heavy velvet curtains, antique gold in colour. Walls of the palest cream. A full grand piano, almost lost in one corner of the room. Did he play? Surely not. But why not? And why had she had preconceived ideas? What had she expected, actually? That his Knightsbridge home would resemble Rose Cottage?

She turned to look at him, her mouth opening and closing wordlessly. 'I—I'm—I have a confession to make.'

'Then make it,' he encouraged, bending to kiss the tip of her nose, enjoying the look on her face.

'Well, I—when I walked into this room, when I got past the shock of it, I thought it didn't suit you. I mean, I thought the room belied the man. Or maybe the man—oh, I don't know what I mean! It's just . . . nothing like I expected, not that I'd actually *thought* about it.' She laughed at herself, looking up at him, vivid green eyes sparkling clearly. 'Show me the rest of it, please, Dominik!'

He gave her an exaggerated look of puzzlement and shrugged. 'With pleasure. But give me a clue, would you? Does all that mean you hate it or you like it?'

'Like it? I *love* it!'

'What?' asked Kirsty, marching confidently towards them. 'What do you love? Not that thing,' she said, pointing at the ceiling—pointing at an exquisite crystal chandelier. 'Everyone likes that thing, but I can't see what all the fuss is about. It's only a big, fancy light. Uncle Nik's fiancée used to think——'

'Kirsty, I'm going to show Diane the rest of the house—and if you don't want to come, we will manage without you, I'm sure. But if you do want to come, behave yourself.' He spoke his last two words very meaningfully, and Kirsty withered slightly while Diane had to fight to suppress laughter. There was no doubt about it, she was a gossip all right.

What had Eve thought about the chandelier?

They moved from room to room with Kirsty trailing two paces behind them like some Arab's wife who knew her place but resented it. She muttered now and then, putting in her twopence-worth when Dominik answered Diane's questions.

'I moved here three years ago. It had been newly decorated but it was way overdue this time, hence my having the decorators in recently. They did a good job, I think.'

'An excellent job,' Diane agreed. In the kitchen she met Nik's housekeeper, which was another surprise. The woman was in her middle forties, unexpectedly youthful and very attractive. Diane spotted the plain gold band on her left hand and wondered, but it was only later that she learned of Mrs Hemmingway's having been widowed when still in her twenties. She had had a series of housekeeping jobs, had been with Dominik in his previous home, also in London, and seemed to have no interest in remarrying or in men at all, for that matter.

Her greeting to Diane was polite but detached, giving the impression that she had been through this same routine countless times before. Did her employer always show his girlfriends around his home? Diane wondered. She had not, not for one minute, forgotten a remark Kirsty had made about Uncle Nik having 'hundreds' of girlfriends. Nor, on the other hand, had she forgotten the pleasure she'd felt this evening, when Kirsty had blabbed about her uncle's not having been out with anyone since meeting her.

It was only when they were back in the drawing-room, when Nik was pouring drinks, that Diane remarked on the contrast between this house and Rose Cottage. Here the bar was set into a wall, cunningly disguised as a cupboard. But it was one which swung out into the room when opened, revealing a store of bottles and glasses of all shapes and sizes, making his stock at the cottage look minuscule by comparison.

'It was hardly home from home for you at the cottage, Dominik. How did it really feel, roughing it like that?'

Though she had asked the question laughingly, he answered her seriously. 'Roughing it? My darling girl, what *do* you think of me, I wonder?' He gestured around the room, but it was a gesture without pride or conceit. 'I wasn't born into these sort of surroundings. Like your own father, mine was comfortably off but not rich. I, however, was always ambitious.'

He said no more and Diane admired him for that. He had become rich, he had made it by himself, but he neither needed nor wished actually to say so in as many words.

'That's why he isn't married,' Kirsty put in. 'My mum used to say he had no time for a wife because he works so hard.'

'Worked, past tense.' Dominik glanced at Diane, acknowledging, as she did, this mention of Kirsty's mother. 'I don't work the hours I used to work, Kirsty, you know that.'

'I know. Because you think you're getting old. Well, I suppose you are.'

'Do you, indeed? Well, you impertinent young madam, you'd better think again. I take it easier than I used to simply because my priorities have changed.'

Diane caught his drift. He had an eleven-year-old girl to supervise these days; his life was different now and it had been for the past eight months.

That was not what Nik had meant, however, and it was Kirsty who clarified the point. She appealed to him earnestly, with no impertinence this time. 'But you said last week that you were older and wiser, that that's why you don't work as hard as you used to.'

Dominik looked at Diane. 'Do you see what I mean, about the awkward questions she asks?' He was grinning, turning back to his niece with an expression of tenderness mingled with exasperation. 'OK, you're right. I did say that. In fact, you quote me verbatim.'

'What does that mean?'

'Word for word.'

'Thank you, Diane.' He sat next to her on the settee, close enough to make her heart skip a beat, just the one beat. 'I am older and wiser, Kirsty, but that doesn't mean I'm getting *old*.'

'But, Uncle Nik, what do you——'

'Allow me.' Diane turned to the eleven-year-old, saying that which Nik would not say himself. 'Your uncle doesn't need to work as hard as he used to, it's as simple as that. He's in a position now to ease up and have more free time.' She did not add 'some of which is for you' because she wouldn't risk the possibility of Kirsty feeling in any way responsible for the change in her uncle's life-style. This was, no doubt, something which had never occurred to the child, and Dominik would never, ever point it out to her. He would never risk her feeling unwanted—or guilty because perforce his life had changed since her advent into it.

Seeming satisfied, Kirsty delivered her final comment on the subject—but it was one which left both adults feeling excruciatingly uncomfortable. 'Good. Then perhaps you will get married, after all. Perhaps he'll marry you, Diane.'

Silence. Awkward, painful silence. A brief one, broken by Dominik when he told Kirsty to go to the kitchen and fill the ice-bucket.

Dinner was excellent, with melon to start, followed by succulent lamb chops cooked to perfection, served by the housekeeper who impinged on the conversation not at all. She moved deftly and silently, delivering and collecting dishes, leaving it to Dominik to refill wineglasses because he obviously preferred to do it himself. Diane told him she would have no more after her second glass. 'I'm driving, remember?'

'Why not stay here the night?' he asked, his face inscrutable.

Kirsty was all for it, but Diane politely refused, politely but firmly, too. All other considerations aside, this was a big, sturdily built house and, while one could not exactly get lost in it, it was big enough to afford plenty of privacy. Stay the night? In one of the many gorgeous guest-rooms? A nice idea, yes, but then what would happen? Would Dominik be certain to stay away from her door? Hardly.

When Kirsty went to bed at her usual time, it was Diane she asked for. 'I'll kiss you goodnight now, Uncle Nik, because I want Diane to come and tuck me up. I want to talk to her about something and it's private.'

He concurred, looking amused, but by the time Diane rejoined him it was ten o'clock and he was no longer amused. She had been gone for fifty minutes. 'What the hell was going on up there?'

'Girl talk.' Diane avoided his eyes, trying to decide where to sit now she was alone with him. The decision was taken out of her hands.

Dominik read her mind, got up and took hold of her by the shoulders. He steered her firmly to the place she had been in earlier, next to him on the settee. 'There! Where I can reach you,' he added deliberately, wickedly. 'And I'd like to know what sort of girl talk—what sort of girl talk could you possibly have with an eleven——' He broke off, laughing outrageously at the look on her face. 'Oh, that again!'

'No.' Diane was laughing, too, at herself as much as anything else. 'This time it was—well, in my childhood it might have been referred to as the birds and the bees, but . . .' She never did finish the sentence, a fresh bout of laughter prevented that. Children these days were evidently taught a great deal more than she had been taught in school about the facts of life. Nevertheless Kirsty had wanted to be told more about the hows, the whys and the wherefores. Still, Diane had been able to answer her questions with none of the awkwardness her uncle would have displayed.

'I'll just tell Mrs Hemmingway we're ready for our coffee.'

'I'm sorry about that, Nik. Has she been waiting to serve it? I could have done it myself if she's waiting to go off duty.'

'She is, and I offered, and she declined. She's like that, very conscientious, very thorough. A godsend, really. That isn't my niece's opinion of the lady, but you can take my word for it. I don't know what I'd do without her.'

Diane took his word for it, thinking, in silent answer to his last remark, that what he would do without her was anyone's guess. Get a replacement? Get a wife? She cringed, both in memory of Kirsty's speculation that Nik might marry and marry *her*, and at the way she had likened, had *lumped together*, the words housekeeper and wife.

Why had she done that? It was not her opinion that a wife was nothing more than a housekeeper, far from it. It certainly wasn't the way she would think of herself, if she did marry . . .

That was more than enough to send her imagination into orbit and, in the moments while Dominik was out of the room, she went as far as envisaging herself married to him. Eyes closed, she launched into an imaginary future with him and her first mental picture was, shamelessly, one of herself and Nik in bed together. Making love. Waking up and smiling at one another, smiling and then reaching out . . .

Would she continue to work? She wasn't sure. Perhaps part-time, just with one agency. The leatherwear. And there again, perhaps not, because she would want to be free to be with him. As much as he was free, she would want to be. Would she want Mrs Hemmingway to stay on? Certainly she would want a say in the running of the household, if not necessarily all the work involved, and in a house of this size it would be——

And then Dominik was back and her eyes came open. He was asking her whether she felt tired, looking concerned, and she assured him she was not feeling tired.

She was feeling idiotic.

How could she have got so carried away? Dominik Channing was not the marrying kind, in spite of his having once gone as far as getting engaged. What had happened there, really? Having been told that Nik had discovered he 'didn't like Eve' any more was not enough. Diane wanted to know more, because one thing was for certain, there was more to it than that, far more to it.

Mrs Hemmingway appeared a second later, before anything else could be said, bearing a tray of silverware and fine china. Everything was so tasteful in this house, it was a whole new side to Dominik that Diane had not suspected. He liked the good things in life; he had, it seemed, always known what he wanted and gone after it. And achieved it.

A faint smile tugged at her lips when she recalled Kirsty telling her that people said her uncle was dynamic. 'I'll pour the coffee, Mrs Hemmingway. Thank you.'

'And I shall clear away,' Nik added. 'I'll bid you goodnight, Mrs Hemmingway.'

The housekeeper withdrew, treating Diane to a polite but appreciative smile. 'It was nice meeting you, Miss West. I hope to see you again.'

'You will,' Nik told her. 'Goodnight, Mrs Hemmingway.' The moment the woman vanished he turned to Diane, grinning broadly. 'You're not going to believe this, but her husband's name was Ernest.'

It was then that Diane learned about her having been widowed in her twenties. 'That's a shame, Nik. It really is. If she's never looked at a man since, she's obviously a one-man woman. Either that or she's never got over her husband's death. Or is that the same thing?'

'Perhaps.' It was just the one word, but it was spoken so seriously, so intensely, that it brought Diane's head round. She looked at him and wondered what was really going through his mind. 'What—what are you thinking, Dominik?'

'Well, I'm not thinking about Mrs Hemmingway any more, that's for sure. I'm thinking about you.' He leaned back into his corner of the settee, his coffee remaining untouched, watching her carefully as he told her what was really on his mind. 'Diane, I've wondered all along about you. I've wondered why you blow hot and cold——' When she looked away he reached for her, letting his hand rest lightly on her arm. 'No, look at me, I'm serious.'

She knew he was serious; what she didn't know was what he expected of her. Not quite, not exactly. 'You'd better explain that. I don't know what you mean. I really don't,' she added, looking at him again, knowing she had said this to him several times before. 'I mean, what is it you want of me?'

'Nothing,' he said. 'And, of course, everything.' He smiled, but there was no humour in it. 'You know how I feel about you—it's all I can do to keep my hands off you.'

So that was how he felt about her. Naturally she had wondered what he felt, what it was he really felt, exactly. But it boiled down to sex. Well, she could not be offended at that, but . . . but she could be disappointed.

And she was.

'Then let's clarify something once and for all, Dominik. I am not going to have an affair with you.'

Quite what she expected his reaction to be, she had had no time to anticipate. Even so, she did not expect the long and searching look he gave her, she did not expect the minutes of ensuing silence, minutes that felt like hours. At length, eyes searching, he asked, 'Why not?'

'I don't have to explain myself, Nik. I don't have to justify to you any decision I make.'

'I won't argue with that,' he said reasonably, so reasonably that she was feeling foolish again. 'But you might decide to tell me anyway, given that I'm not in any way expecting you to justify yourself. And I'm not, you know, I'm merely curious. That's all, Diane. Can't you trust me, enough to be honest with me?'

She wanted to. Oh, how she wanted to! She wanted to tell him that she was inhibited simply because she had never *had* an affair. But how could she? Firstly he wouldn't believe it; secondly, even if he did, he would no doubt laugh his head off.

It was a horrid moment. Tears sprang to her eyes and she looked away, feeling quite ridiculous—and afraid. Afraid he would sense the truth. He was a very perceptive man, perceptive and sensitive both.

But he did not perceive the truth. He was reaching for her and she stiffened, still unable to look at him. 'Don't, Nik. Please.'

He behaved as if he hadn't heard her, firmly pulling her into his arms and imprisoning her tightly. In an instant his mouth was on hers and he was kissing her not in any demanding way but gently, as if at some level, in some way, he was in sympathy with her. 'Diane,' he murmured, his mouth only a fraction from hers, 'please tell me, talk to me. *Is* there someone else? Or has there been someone else? Someone you loved, someone you're still hankering after? If there is—was, I'll understand. I promise you that. But I would like to know. For my sake, tell me, please.'

Gently she pulled away from him, closing her eyes so he would not see the dismay in them. Oh, damn, was *that* what he thought? It was a million miles from the truth, but—but could she blame him for thinking along these lines? No, of course not! He couldn't know that she was not what she appeared to be. He had wondered why she blew hot and cold, as he'd put it, and so he might. She *had* behaved like that, the memory of their times together in Boscombe was only too fresh in her mind. Images flashed behind her closed eyes, images of herself, flirting with him, if only unwittingly. Stretched out on the beach in a bikini which left nothing to the imagination. The dress she had worn when he had taken her into Bournemouth that evening. Being in his arms and encouraging his lovemaking with everything she had in her. Reaching for him. Moaning softly against his mouth. Reaching for him again when his hands left her body.

Damn! Of course he didn't understand her. How could he?

She gathered herself together, summoning her inner resources in order to get through this difficult moment, which she would do with the truth, the truth as far as it went. 'No, there's no one. Nor has there been. No one I'm carrying a torch for. It's simply this,' she added, turning bravely to look straight into his eyes, 'if you want to continue seeing me——'

'Of course I want that! What do you——?'

'Hear me out, Dominik. If you want to go on seeing me, we have to reach an understanding.'

'I see,' he said cynically. 'You mean it will have to be on your terms.'

'I'd rather not put it like that,' she said, with a façade of calm that successfully hid her true feelings. Inwardly she was afraid this would be it, that he would tell her it was no go . . . which in turn would tell her that her body was the *only* attraction she held for him.

How would she cope, if it did come to that? In any other circumstances she would tell a man to go to hell—but these were not other circumstances. She loved Dominik Channing. On leaving Eden Cottage she had been uncertain, she had tried to persuade herself she was mistaken, but, during the week that followed, all doubts had disappeared. She was in love with him, totally, hopelessly.

It was Dominik who broke their eye-contact this time. He looked away, picked up his coffee-cup with mind racing. He just could not fathom this woman, and he certainly couldn't come to grips with this new twist in the game she was obviously still playing. Wasn't she? Or was it merely that he was rushing her? Maybe she was less experienced than he'd thought? Oh, he was aware that she was not all she appeared to be, he had been all along, but—could it be that simple? Maybe, just maybe, all he needed was to give her time. 'All right,' he said, 'you can take it that we have an understanding, Diane.'

CHAPTER EIGHT

DOMINIK was as good as his word, at least to begin with, but he never missed an opportunity to tease Diane when he could or to take her in his arms and kiss her into a frenzy of yearning, until she was almost senseless.

Almost, but not quite, senseless. Diane established the ground rules for their continuing relationship immediately, on the night of the party at his prospective customer's home in Tonbridge. Without a shadow of a doubt she knew she must not let things go as far as they had that night in Rose Cottage. If she did that would be it, and *it* would mean the beginning of the end with Dominik, of that she felt certain, too. And yet . . . he seemed to enjoy her company; it seemed he really did like her for *herself*.

'Wow!' This was his greeting when she opened her door to him on the Saturday of the party. Quite deliberately she had chosen—bought, at considerable expense—a full-length dress which could only be described as demure. It was sleeveless, with cut-away shoulders, it was the exact green shade of her eyes, and it was simplicity itself. Nevertheless, Dominik put a different interpretation on her appearance. 'Now *that* is gorgeous. It leaves quite a lot to the imagination—but as you know, I have a vivid imagination, Diane . . .'

What could she do but laugh? She laughed because, with him, she definitely couldn't win! Not when he saw such mystery in a fully-clothed female body . . .

'What time are we due?' she asked in an effort to distract

him. 'The party, Dominik, the party.'

'Oh. Yes. Any time. In other words, there's time for me to come in and have a drink with you here, just a small one.'

'No, we'll go.' Diane went immediately for the wrap which she had also had to buy because she possessed nothing else suitable to go with the evening dress.

It was already eight-thirty and his car was outside the main door of the building, newly washed and gleaming dark red in the vanishing light. As he always had, he saw her seated comfortably before moving round to the driver's seat. 'I forgot to ask you last night, how was business this past week?'

'Sluggish,' she said without concern. 'It'll pick up come September and we'll really take off during October and November.'

'And December, surely? For Christmas?'

'December's always interesting inasmuch as one never knows what to expect. Usually things slacken off drastically during the middle of the month because buyers don't like to make repeat orders unless they're certain of selling, so when it gets that close to Christmas, with the end of the season and the January sales in mind, they'll keep their orders to a minimum, except for specials, of course.'

'So January will be a quiet month for you?'

'Very, and the first half of February.'

'It would be a good time to take a holiday then, get some sunshine abroad.'

'I've thought of doing that. I'll have to wait and see.' She didn't notice the half-smile on his face, he hadn't taken his eyes off the road. It was only when he went on that she realised what he had in mind, why he had asked about January and business.

'Maybe we could go away together—at my expense, of

course.'

The look Diane gave him was calculated to have a shrivelling effect. It was water off a duck's back, however. 'You,' she said, 'are incorrigible.'

His retort came smoothly, his eyes holding a brief caress as they swept over her. 'Not at all. I simply know what I want and go for it. And I want you, Diane West. But then, what else is new?'

She was laughing again; he had the ability to do that to her, even at moments such as this. By the time they got to the party the conversation had changed entirely and they were thrashing out a difference of opinion over something that had been on the news that evening.

Suddenly they were at the house; they had passed a golf course, then some woods, and they were turning into a long, gently curving driveway at the bottom of which was a vast but very graceful building.

It was Diane's turn to say 'wow', which she did.

Dominik smiled. 'The home of Mr Emile Prendergast, property speculator. I may or may not be doing a deal with him on some of the properties I want to shed. You'll like him,' he added, drawing the Mercedes to a halt on the crunching gravel, parking it amid dozens of other cars at the back of the house. 'He's a very charming man—but ruthless, make no mistake!'

Diane saw nothing of the man's ruthlessness, only his charm. She and Dominik were ushered indoors by a uniformed maid, no less, and taken through to a drawing-room buzzing with conversations, full of glamorous-looking, beautifully dressed people. But she was not overawed; she and Dominik made a striking couple, she in her sophisticated simplicity, with her hair swept up into a loose knot, make-up immaculate but soft, her only adornment being the ear-rings and the watch she was wearing. As for Dominik—well, many heads turned to look at him, male and female, looking magnificent as he did in his formal evening suit, bow-tie and gleaming white shirt. Against the contrast of the tan he had so easily acquired on the south coast, his shirt looked almost iridescent. Tall and broad, not lacking charm himself, he was smiling at the man who came quickly to greet him and Diane, and she felt proud to be on his arm.

She was introduced to Emile Prendergast and was drawn with Dominik into the circle of people from whom their host had broken away to greet them.

Within half an hour she was sipping at a second glass of champagne, taken from one of the trays being constantly circulated by waiters and waitresses, and she was wishing she could sit down. The conversation around her was by no means over her head, but it was somewhat boring because the group were talking about people she had never met. She wondered whether there would be any music later—or was it not that sort of party? It was certainly of a type she had never been to before, not in such surroundings, not with these sort of people.

'I can see why you weren't very enthusiastic about coming here, Nik.' She muttered this to him when the circle changed at one point, when new people came to join it and others drifted away to natter elsewhere.

He laughed aloud, pulling his voice in with an effort to whisper, 'Are you bored, darling?'

'Well . . . not exactly, no. I just wish I could sit down.'

'Then sit down, by all means.' With a smile and a wave at the others, he steered Diane away. 'And I'll bet you'd like something to eat?'

'Yes, there's that, too!' She laughed; she had had nothing

to eat, having taken it for granted there would be plenty of food at the party.

And there was. And then some! The spread in the dining-room was everything she might have known it would be; there was nothing she could possibly fancy that was not there, from the most delicate of appetisers right through to beautifully presented desserts. She brightened up and picked up a plate from the end of the table.

'There'll be dancing later, indoors and out,' Dominik said, seeming delighted by her new-found contentment.

'Really?'

'Oh, yes. Don't let appearances deceive you, Diane. A lot of them look like stuffed shirts, but they're not. Wait till they've had time to drink a bit more and the place will hot up considerably, you'll see.'

She saw—she saw a lot. As the evening wore on, some voices got louder, some shriller—and some a little slurred. Where the atmosphere had been rather subdued to begin with, by eleven o'clock it was gay. And it was warmer in the house. Dozens of people were outdoors on the lawns, milling around with drinks or just posing with them; some were dancing on a paved patio on one end of which was a sextet hired especially for the occasion.

That was where Dominik and Diane were, on the patio, dancing their first dance and discovering how well they did this together when their host suddenly interrupted them.

Emile Prendergast was about fifty years old, and a widower, she had learned. He was nearly as tall as Nik and, though he did not possess the younger man's beauty, he was very handsome and most distinguished, with his silver-grey waves and a very erect, near-arrogant deportment. He was also looking at Diane with eyes bordering on the flirtatious. 'I claim,' he said, with a neutral glance towards Dominik, 'all my rights as your host.'

Diane eyed him with more speculation than she let show. 'And what exactly are they, Mr Prendergast?'

'Oh, Emile, please! To dance with you, the most attractive woman at the party.'

She glanced at Dominik, unsure of herself and equally unsure of her host. Had he had too much to drink? She caught the glint of amusement in Nik's eyes and took that as her lead; he clearly did not mind this interruption. 'And so you shall,' she said smoothly, smilingly, to her host. 'But I'll bet you've said that to *all* the girls . . .'

There was a bark of laughter from Nik. He slapped his host on the shoulder, shaking his head. 'And she would win her bet, eh? OK, Emile, I shall go and find something long and cold and non-alcoholic to drink and you shall dance with Diane. Just the one,' he added, laughing again as he departed.

It was easy enough, Emile was a good dancer and he held her at a very respectable distance. He thanked her, and Dominik when he reappeared, and moved on to the next most attractive woman at the party.

Back in Dominik's arms, and not being held at a respectable distance, Diane remarked on how right he had been. 'He is charming. Very.'

'He's half-French,' he told her, by way of explanation.

She laughed at that. 'And a widower. It's a pity my stepmother didn't meet him instead of my father, she'd have loved getting her mitts on a house like this.'

'Oh, *naughty*!' He pulled her closer, as if he would punish her. 'Wicked girl! I've a good mind to put you over my knee for a crack like that.'

'What? Here? Now?' She laughed up at him defiantly, her eyes challenging because she knew how safe she was—

or thought she knew.

'Don't tempt me.' He smiled into her eyes, his face only inches from hers, his breath a cool and vaguely minty breeze against her mouth. 'And stop looking at me like that, you minx, because that's a provocation in itself, and if you don't want a public demonstration . . .' He left the rest unsaid, drawing her even closer as the music changed, became more smoochy, so that she became quite shockingly aware of every contour of his body from his chest to his thighs.

She took the point—she could hardly miss it. 'All right, Nik, ease up, will you? I don't want a public demonstration—of any kind.'

His laughter was a soft, low and utterly seductive rumble against her ear. 'Then why don't we call it a day? Let's go home and make love.'

It was odd, she thought, how his words of themselves could create that certain yearning in her. Let's go home and make love. Such a simple sentence, such a delicious prospect! Much of her longed to say yes, fine, my place or yours? Much of her but not all of her; common sense still prevailed, common sense and, yes, in the circumstances a certain amount of distaste. She could just imagine it: at three o'clock in the morning he would slip out of her bed to get dressed, to be home in time for Kirsty waking up in the morning, so there would be no questions asked. Or vice versa, if she were to go to his home.

'Well,' she said, smiling up at him but with no encouragement whatever, 'I wouldn't mind going home.'

They did just that. And, when they got to the main door of the building, Dominik insisted on going upstairs with her. She insisted there was no need for that, that she would be perfectly all right going up to her flat alone.

He won.

'Give me your key,' he said when they were standing outside her front door. 'I just want to see that everything's all right in there.'

Everything was all right. Diane turned to him. 'No! Don't take your jacket off, you're not staying.'

'Oh, come *on*! Just a cup of coffee——'

'No. And I mean no, Nik.'

She won.

During September business increased steadily, and October was a busy month for Diane. She loved every minute of it, in spite of being unable to see much of Dominik. He never complained that she was out of the area so much, though she herself sometimes resented it, much as she liked her work. She liked meeting so many people, buyers and assistants and customers; she liked her meetings with her principals and the excitement when they produced new samples for new ranges, the garments she would take orders for for the forthcoming season.

During October she saw Nik only five times, though, an average of once a week. It happened that sometimes when she was available, he wasn't because he was dining with someone or other on matters of business. Or so he said. How could she know, really? Yet she tended to believe him because there was no longer any doubt in her mind that he really did like her for herself, very much so.

When he rang to tell her they had been invited by Emile Prendergast to a Hallowe'en party, which was to be held on the Saturday, he also told her it would be something of a celebration for him personally. 'We've concluded a deal with which we're both extremely satisfied, Diane. So I think it would be nice to accept his invitation, don't you?'

'Certainly! It's nice of him to ask us. I mean, you don't really mix much with him socially, do you?'

'Not if I can help it,' he admitted, a smile in his voice. Diane knew his preference for quieter evenings, for candlelit dinners in romantic settings, at least with her. He had always taken her to such places thus far, driving out of London to the many places he knew, and to one or two which were untried.

For the following week they had already made two definite dates for the theatre, for new shows they were both wanting to see—but the party he was now talking about was on this coming Saturday, just five days away. 'Well, it's fine by me, Nik. Sounds fun.'

'It isn't being held at his house, by the way. It's at a country club on the other side of Tonbridge. Anyway, if I don't see you before then, I'll pick you up at seven, OK? It's a sit-down meal, hence the early start.'

He was about to hang up but she told him to hold on. 'I had a letter from Kirsty this morning, she answered mine by return of post and——'

'You're still writing to her at school?'

'Of course I am. She's missing Penny, she says.'

'She's probably missing her dog more than she misses me.' Dominik laughed and then sobered suddenly. 'You do realise that she might just end up living with me permanently, don't you? I mean, that this place might be her home.'

'I know what you mean. But so what? That's not a dreadful prospect to you, surely?'

'No.' There was a pause. 'No, not at all.'

Diane glanced at the receiver after she had put it down, wondering what had really been going through Nik's mind.

She didn't see him before Saturday. She was ready and

waiting at seven, dressed appropriately for the bitterly cold evening it was, full-length coat and all. Under it she had on what she hoped would be an appropriate dress, a fairly casual effort in what they called 'winter white'. Cashmere. A total cover-up. Dominik would like it.

Of course there was no way of knowing, as she got into his car, that this evening would prove disastrous. How could she know that? How could she know, any more than Nik did, that during the latter part of the evening his fiancée, his *ex*-fiancée, would come drifting into Emile's private party with two men in tow?

Eve Montgomery did just that. The first Diane knew of her presence, realising immediately who this woman was, was when she sidled up to where they were sitting with an over-effusive and slightly drunken, 'Nik, darling! How *lovely* to see you! How *are* you?'

Diane saw the entire picture at once. One of the woman's entourage had gone over to Emile, was shaking hands and laughing with him, obviously a friend and quite a close one, by the look of it. As for Eve, she merely glanced over her shoulder at the party's host and gave a little wave. Not a close friend, perhaps no more than an acquaintance, via the man, no doubt.

Diane observed it all, and Dominik returned the woman's greeting with a blandness bordering on the impolite. 'Eve, how've you been? Let me introduce you to Diane.'

Introductions were made. Eve's hand came out and touched briefly with Diane's, but her eyes were scanning Diane with an intense and all-consuming thoroughness. She missed nothing, not that Diane cared one way or the other.

Within a moment she drifted away, given no encouragement to linger either from Dominik or Diane. But, oh! Diane was curious. The woman Dominik had once been engaged to was beautiful, as blonde as Diane was black-haired. Similar build, similar height, but that was the end of their similarity. Eve was truly sophisticated, very confident of herself and her ability to impress. Emile Prendergast was drinking in the sight of her—he had never stopped doing so—but, now she had moved down to his end of the long table, he seemed quite mesmerised by her.

'So that's Eve.' Quietly, to Dominik.

'That's Eve.' He was watching Diane's reaction carefully.

'She's beautiful, Nik.'

'Very. But it's a question of appearances again, my darling. I regret having to say it, but Eve's beauty is skin-deep. Listen, are you comfortable with this situation or would you rather leave?'

Leave? Why should she? Why should she want to leave? But what of Dominik? Perhaps he disliked—or even hated—the situation. 'Not at all, I'm enjoying myself. But what about you? If you find this difficult——'

'*Difficult?*' He laughed, shortly, without mirth. 'No, Diane. She hasn't got that much power. I've told you, she's as good as invisible to me.'

But she was not invisible to Diane, or rather Diane was not invisible to Eve, for when she went into the ladies' room some twenty minutes later Diane was followed. Followed, pursued and subjected to a dose of verbal poison.

'Ah, Miss West!' Eve Montgomery timed it nicely, appearing just as Diane was washing her hands. She came over to the basins, smiling, weaving slightly, and draped herself in what would have been a fascinating pose to male eyes.

'Miss Montgomery? You wanted to talk to me?'

'Oh, but how formal we're being!' She reached out to touch Diane's shoulder, a patronising gesture that thankfully lasted only a second. 'I'm Eve and you are Diane. I am the old and you are the new, if you follow my drift.'

'I'm afraid I don't.' Diane fished in her bag for her compact. 'So perhaps you'll get to the point.'

'The point?' Definitely drunk, she was definitely under the influence. 'Oh, yes. It's simple really, I just want to give you a word of warning. One girl to another, you know. About Dominik Channing. I can speak from considerable experience, you see.'

Diane did not doubt that, and it would have been so easy to say so, but she resisted because it was not really a temptation. Bitchiness added to bitchiness could only make more of its kind.

Eve got to the point. 'I don't know what stage you're at in your relationship with Nik—but I hear from a certain party who will remain unnamed that you've been in his orbit for at least a month. And that, my dear, is about par for the course. It wasn't in my case, but then Dominik and I were going to take things as far as the altar—until I called it off.'

Not for one moment did Diane's hand waver; she was applying lipstick and she did it as well as she always did it, but her eyes shot of their own accord to look at Eve via the mirrors over the basins. *She* had called off the engagement? Was it true? Diane had always assumed that Dominik had been the one to finish that relationship. Perhaps she shouldn't have assumed; perhaps this was yet another case where she had made false assumptions. Perhaps this was the reason for Nik's . . . bitterness wasn't the right word . . . for his insistence that Eve no longer existed.

'Anyway,' Eve Montgomery was saying, 'I only wanted to warn you that when the novelty you are to Nik wears off, it'll be over between you. I know his track record very well indeed. So let me see, when he's been to bed with you on . . . how many occasions shall we say . . .?'

'I think enough has been said, Miss Montgomery. More than enough. I have followed your drift, but I'm not about to thank you for the warning because this is none of your business.' How she managed not to shout at the woman, Diane didn't know. She was fuming, so angry it was all she could do to put her make-up back in her bag and close the catch, her hands were shaking so much.

She made a dignified exit without looking back, without knowing whether Eve was following her.

Dominik, alerted at once by the look on her face, got to his feet and pulled her chair out for her. 'What is it, Diane? You look—are you feeling ill? Sit down, darling.'

'I'm not ill, I'm just angry.'

'About what?'

'Not now, Dominik. Just take me home, please. *Now.*'

She refused point-blank to talk to him in the car, not out of stubbornness but because she literally could not talk. Incensed by Eve Montgomery's audacity, the only consolation she could feel from that encounter was in the knowledge that she herself had behaved with dignity. As for Dominik—she turned to glance at him, wondering whether she really knew him. *Had* he lied to her, not directly but by implication, which was just as bad? And, if Eve had been the one to break off their engagement, why had she done it? What did she know about Dominik that would make her want to break it off?

'I don't know what's going on with you,' he said quietly, 'but if you look at me with that sort of venom one more time, Diane, I'm going to stop this car and shake the story out of you. So why don't you just spit it out, now? It has something to do with Eve, hasn't it?'

Diane didn't answer, nor did she look again, because he might well carry out his threat.

The instant they were in the privacy of her flat, she let go, unable to sit down, still shaking a little. 'Your ex-fiancée followed me into the ladies', Dominik, and what she had to say to me was both distasteful and revealing! For one thing, she said it was she who broke off your engagement!'

'And for another?' He was unruffled, unperturbed, comfortable on her settee, his feet on a matching ottoman.

'Never mind that! Is it true? Did she break off your engagement?'

'What difference does it make? What does it matter?'

Diane's heart sank. So he had lied, albeit by implication. The wind went out of her sails and she sat, going on to tell him, because she saw no reason not to, of all the other things Eve had said. Nothing spared, nothing added.

Dominik listened without interruption and, when it was obvious she had finished, he rounded on her, swinging his feet to the floor and hurling himself to a standing position. 'Right! First things first, Diane. Have I ever lied to you? Come on, answer me!'

'I—I—not to my knowledge.'

'Furthermore, why should I lie? Consider that. I have nothing to hide—from you or from anyone else. Now there's no way that I am going to defend myself against that vituperation, because you yourself are going to decide about Eve and all that she said to you. I am merely going to point out to you that the woman was drunk, as in *plastered*.'

'I know. But I——'

'You know? Oh, I see, you knew but you still took to heart what she said to you?'

Diane looked at him helplessly. He was right. 'Well, not really——'

He was not going to let her off easily. 'That's not good enough. You were looking daggers at me in the car, and by the time we got back here I'd been tried, judged and sentenced.'

'Dominik——'

'I haven't finished. Since you're clearly incapable of thinking logically tonight, I can see that I shall have to point out to you also that you and I have never been to bed together. Yet here I stand, three months into my celibate relationship with you.' Loving you, he almost added. He might have said it, too, had the realisation not hit him like a thunderbolt. Instead he turned his back to her, not knowing what to say next.

'Dominik? Look, I'm sorry, but please try to see my point of view. You've never told me what happened with Eve, you never actually said who finished it, or why.'

'You never asked,' he said, fencing and realising it. He needed time, a moment in which to think. Loving her. *Did* he love her? Was it real, or was she merely driving him slowly out of his mind from wanting her so much?

'Well, I am asking now.' Diane spoke softly, not wanting to antagonise him further, not wanting him to interpret her words as a demand.

To her relief, he turned around and sat down again. 'I'm not angry with you,' he said, 'I'm disappointed because you let Eve get to you like that. You should know me better.'

She did, and she was not pleased with herself. Maybe she was just insecure, vulnerable because she loved him so much, but there was no sign whatever of his feeling the same way about her.

Silence reigned. It was neither awkward nor uncomfortable, it was just a silence.

Diane got to her feet. 'Shall I—would you like a cup of coffee?'

'I would. Very much.'

She made two mugs of instant, one with milk and one without. Wordlessly, she put the black coffee on a table near Dominik, almost jumping when he spoke suddenly. 'Eve and I split up because of Kirsty.'

'*Kirsty*? But why? How——'

His face broke into a smile, so full and genuine that it startled her. 'You would react like that, wouldn't you, Diane? It would never occur to you that Kirsty could be the cause of a broken engagement.'

She didn't understand and she admitted it. 'You don't mean . . . you can't mean that she mixed things between you and Eve? With her gossip?'

Nik actually laughed at that, her best guess. 'No, I do not. You really are incredibly sweet at times. What gossip? See what I mean? Some of Eve's propaganda is still sticking to you! And take two seconds to think about what you just said, ask yourself what sort of relationship I would have had with Eve if gossip from a little girl could have ruined it. It would hardly have been of the stuff necessary to build a marriage on, would it?'

'All right, so I said something stupid. But what else—what *was* it?'

'Nothing complicated. Eve simply showed her true colours when I told her there was every probability that Kirsty would be living with us when we married.'

Diane looked blank, unwittingly endearing herself to him even further. He watched her face, saw her lack of comprehension and knew in that moment that he had not mistaken what he felt for her. He loved her, he loved her very, very much. 'You still don't get it, do you, darling?'

'I'm just beginning to. Eve doesn't like children, right?'

In a mannerism all too familiar to her he shrugged, held up a hand. 'Whether she would like to have children of her own I don't know. She led me to believe she would, during the course of our relationship. But she absolutely did not want to take charge of someone else's child. While my sister was in the hospital during her last few weeks, Kirsty was with me. Eve knew all about the situation with Philip Nolan, his unreliability, or at least his unreliability as I then assumed it, and when I said to her in as many words that Kirsty would naturally live with me, and continue to do so if her father stayed abroad, Eve gave me the benefit of her finest tantrum. I'd seen glimpses of them before—but nothing like the one she treated me to on that particular occasion. She said to me, and I quote: "There is no way, and I mean no way that I'm going to take on that little brat, Nik." Kirsty had,' he added, 'been a little difficult to have around just at that time.'

'For heaven's sake, of course she had! Her mother was in the hospital, dying!'

'Quite so. Crystal-clear, isn't it? Easy for you to see—or any other reasonable human being, for that matter.'

But not Eve. Diane said no more, she didn't need to. She wasn't going to put Eve down, she wasn't going to judge her. The woman was just . . . who she was. But who she was was not right for Dominik Channing. How he'd got as far as being engaged to her, Diane did not know. But that didn't matter, either. It was all in the past, all part and parcel of his being older and wiser, as he had put it to Kirsty a few weeks ago. Kirsty! Poor mite. Thank heavens she was enjoying her new school, really, truly enjoying it.

Nor did it matter whether Eve had walked out on Dominik or whether he had told her to go, though she knew in her heart what had actually happened. He would have told Eve what he thought of her, he would have given her a piece of his mind in no uncertain terms.

She looked over at him, understanding him far better than she had before. Far better. He was not only sensitive but honourable, a good man whose feelings ran deep. He had a strong sense of justice, of fair play, and, although Eve had spoken quite appallingly about him, he had not done the same about her. He had merely quoted her, pointing out only, as far as the exchange in the ladies' room was concerned, the fact that she had had too much to drink.

Diane understood, now, why he regarded her simply as not existing any more.

'Diane? Where have you gone? I was saying that it's time I made tracks.'

'You're going?'

'Well, that is another way of putting it, yes.' He smiled at her, reaching for his jacket, wondering whether she might just encourage him to stay.

No such luck. She was talking about tomorrow and looking uncomfortable for some reason.

'Nik, I forgot to tell you. My father rang this morning, asking me to invite you to dinner tomorrow, and I accepted on your behalf. I hope that was all right? I mean, I know Mrs Hemmingway is normally off on Sundays so——'

'That's fine.' She was standing just two feet away from him, her beautiful green eyes doing their witchery quite without knowing it. He wanted to kiss her but he wouldn't, he wouldn't because a certain scepticism had risen in him during this past half-hour or so, because he had been talking about Eve, no doubt. But what of Diane? Was there something he had yet to discover about her that would bring a similar disillusionment? Did he, perhaps, not really understand women as well as he had thought he did?

Diane leaned against her front door when he had gone, feeling wretched. She had explained to Nik that in her father's house dinner on Sundays really meant a late lunch. Eating at around two or two-thirty. And he had smiled and nodded and said that would be nice, that he would collect her at one-thirty, so they could drive together to the bungalow he had not yet visited. So tomorrow would be his first meeting with her father and her stepmother. She ought to be glad, but she felt nothing.

Why had he gone without so much as kissing her, without touching her in even the smallest way? And why, *why*, had he looked so downhearted?

CHAPTER NINE

IT WASN'T until lunch was almost finished that Annabel broke the news which was something of a bombshell to Diane. They were in the middle of eating her home-made apple pie with cream when she suddenly looked up. 'Oh, I forgot to tell you, Diane, I got myself a job last week. Just part-time.'

'Really?' Too much emphasis, she was letting her shock show. Well, perhaps that was only fair, because it looked as if she really had misjudged this pretty woman who was her stepmother. Quite apart from this revelation, there were many indications that she was proving to be, and would continue to be, a good wife to Frank West. Not only was the house spotlessly clean, it had also been made cosier by Annabel's rearrangement of the furniture and the addition of one or two bits and pieces.

She also cooked and baked superbly, insistent on making her own bread since she now had the time to do so. As for Diane's father, the man simply looked as if he'd been given a new lease of life, he was unmistakably happy and content, as was his new stepson, Bobby. And now this—Annabel going out to work when she did not need to. 'How come? I mean, I thought you enjoyed being at home.'

'Oh, I do. But not all the time, I've discovered. With Frank at work and Bobby in school—well, I thought a part-time job might be nice. Mornings only, so I can be here and organised when Bobby and Frank come home.'

Dominik, who had made a hit with them during the first

five minutes of his arrival, looked across the table at Diane and winked mischievously. What it really meant, of course, was, *'See?'* Had it been appropriate to do so, she would have pulled a face at him.

But it wasn't appropriate, and furthermore Diane really didn't know whether Dominik's good mood was purely for the benefit of Frank and Annabel or whether it was genuine. When he had collected her from her flat earlier he had been subdued, hardly talking on the drive over here. She had asked him what was wrong and had been told, 'Nothing.'

Something was wrong, though, between them. Wasn't it? Or was he still put out about last night's episode with Eve Montgomery? Was it that, or was it something more? Diane smiled to herself, not because she was feeling happy but at her own thoughts: she wanted to be alone with Nik, and wouldn't he regard that as a turn up for the books!

She found she had to wait quite a time for the opportunity to be alone with him, however, because as soon as the table was cleared and the dishwasher stacked, her father asked whether anyone fancied a game of Scrabble, and everyone including Dominik reacted with enthusiasm at the idea. One game inevitably led to two, and when at last the board was put away it was only because Bobby's bedtime had arrived.

As open and demonstrative as ever, he kissed everyone in the room, Dominik, too, stranger or no stranger, and scooted off happily.

'He's a credit to you,' Nik told Annabel, who responded with blatant pleasure and pride. 'You've done a good job—and it was single-handed for the most part, wasn't it?'

Diane watched this exchange with interest, seeing no hint at all of Annabel flirting with Nik in even the smallest way.

But she might have, because he was, after all, not only her contemporary but also beautiful and charming. But there was nothing in her eyes or in her body-language to indicate an attraction towards Dominik and Diane was mightily relieved to see this, not because she felt proprietorial towards Dominik but because it was to her yet another indication of how wrong she had been about her father's new young wife.

'For the most part,' she was saying to Nik. 'He was very young when his father and I split up.' She said nothing more, knowing it was not expected of her.

Diane had told her father and Annabel only a little about Dominik: that he was in the property business, unmarried but with his niece in his charge. She had not told them she was in love with him, though they no doubt had their own ideas on the matter, given that her relationship with him was now into its fourth month. Just. But that was quite a long time for Diane, as her father knew, of course. Since leaving school she had had a lot of boyfriends, but they had all been short-lived friendships.

By the time she and Dominik were able to extract themselves—extraction was what it felt like to her, if not to him—it was turned ten o'clock. He thanked her father and Annabel for a splendid meal and an enjoyable time, saying he hoped to see them again.

'Of course you'll see us again,' Frank said confidently. 'And quite soon, I hope.'

'What are you doing for Christmas?' This came from Annabel, and they all started laughing because Christmas was seven weeks away.

Dominik was quick to tease her about it. 'I see! You'd like us to meet again soon, but not until Christmas, is that it?'

She was shaking her head, laughing, her blonde curls

moving attractively. 'I didn't mean that at all, and you know it! No, it was just a thought—I mean, I wondered——' She broke off, glancing uncertainly at Diane.

'Well, I'll be here, of course, but I can't speak for Dominik.' The subject of Christmas had never been discussed, except in reference to Kirsty's father and a possible party. But who knew what her relationship with Dominik would be by then? Certainly not her. In any case, her father would be taking it for granted that she would be at home with him, at least for Christmas Day.

'I do have plans,' Nik said to Annabel, with a polite hint of apology in his voice. 'My niece will be home for the holidays and her father is coming back to England to settle after a long stint abroad.'

'Oh, yes, I—Diane did mention that, but I'd forgotten. Anyhow, we'll see you before then.'

'Indeed you will. And thank you again.'

He drove Diane home through a torrential downpour, and stunned her by declining her offer of coffee.

'I—you don't want to come up?' He had stopped outside the main entrance so she should have realised; had he wanted to go inside he would have parked in a legitimate place, round the side of the building.

'I'm tired, Diane.' He looked at her, smiling, no apparent moodiness, but she didn't believe him.

'Tired? On a Sunday?'

'Can't people get tired on Sundays?' He laughed both outwardly and inwardly, questioning his own sanity in refusing this offer to be alone with her. But he had hardly slept the night before. The business with Eve, and in particular Diane's initial reaction to it, had bothered him more than he had realised. Diane remained an unknown quantity in some ways, not least in that he really did not know how she felt about him. 'I'm sorry, what did you just say, Diane?'

'You see, you are preoccupied. Not tired, just preoccupied. Are you still angry because I doubted you, about the Eve thing?'

'I wasn't angry with you, I told you that last night.'

'Then kiss me,' she said, laughing when she saw his eyebrows shoot up. 'Why so surprised? All I want is a goodnight kiss!'

Which was fine, except that it developed into the sort that could so easily become a good morning kiss, the sort that neither of them wanted ever to end, the kind of kiss that failed to satisfy because it created a need for more. And more. And it was Dominik who called a halt.

'We're sitting in a very public place,' he reminded her, his breathing heavy and laboured. He reached for her hand, his own hand shaking somewhat. 'Does your offer still stand? I'll come up——'

She shook her head, eyes closed against the blasting she felt would be inevitable. She knew very well what she had just done, because the effect on her had been identical. Oh, how she wanted him! So why, *why* didn't she just say yes? 'No.'

There was no telling off. He merely nodded, as if he had known what she would say. 'Hot and cold again, Diane. But it can't go on, you do realise that, I suppose?'

'I'm . . . sorry.'

'I doubt that,' he said, at the same time opening his door to let her out of the car. Oblivious to the rain, he stood, taking her face in his hands. 'We have a date for Tuesday, remember. Would you like to eat before or after the theatre?'

Her mind zipped to Wednesday morning and where she

planned to be. She had to make an early start. 'Before. I'll be going out of London on Wednesday morning.'

The rest of November whizzed by. Diane's travelling was made difficult during the last week of it by an early snowfall. Nevertheless, she kept on the move and saw as many customers as she could. But she was enjoying herself less and less as time moved on, because her work all too often kept her from Dominik, either because she was too shattered to see him during the week or because she was out of town, alone in a hotel room. With time to think. Always about him. Sometimes she would ring him just to hear his voice, not necessarily because she had something to say.

And then, blissfully, business went into its predictable decline because it was the middle of December and Christmas was approaching fast. As to that, Christmas itself, her plans to be with her family had not changed—and Nik's plans had become more certain. Kirsty was home for the holidays, just, and the party she had suggested for her father was going to happen on Boxing Day. Boxing Day had been Nik's idea, in order to give Philip Nolan a couple of days to recover from his journey and to get reacquainted with his daughter. And with Dominik, too.

'It's going to be interesting, having him under my roof,' he said to Diane during the evening three days before Christmas.

'In what way?' She was in his living-room, which she still enjoyed so much, having just settled Kirsty for the night. Mrs Hemmingway had excelled herself with dinner tonight and Diane was feeling mellow. Strains of Beethoven, Nik's favourite composer, also becoming Diane's, were emanating softly from the speakers in two corners of the big room, and in the hearth there was the soft flicker of reflected firelight. It was not, alas, a real fire but one of those wonderful gas lookalikes which almost passed as the genuine article.

And in front of the hearth lay Penny, perfectly still from the tip of her nose to the tip of her tail—except for the occasional twitch of an ear. Eyes closed. Sleeping, or at least appearing to be. Diane smiled contentedly, turning to look at Dominik who was close beside her on the settee, his arm draped around her shoulder. The crystal chandelier was not on; the only light in the room was that of several lamps, table and standard, and in this soft glow he looked more darkly beautiful than ever. As she looked at him in that particular instant, her heart contracted with a mixture of joy at the sheer loveliness of this moment and with a definite yet indefinable fear for the future. She and Nik were not lovers in the accepted sense of the word, not lovers but—what? Friends? Put simply, she was wondering, really, what the New Year would hold in store . . . for her, for him . . . for them both.

'Getting to know the man he is today,' he said in answer to her question, though as if she needn't have asked. 'He was only here for a couple of days at the time of Jane's death. So I can't say I know how his mind works these days.'

'Oh. Then I see what you mean.'

'And it isn't impossible,' he went on, looking at her with what seemed to her an odd expression in his eyes, 'that things won't work out with him and Kirsty. I'm not being pessimistic, Diane, I'm only saying that Philip might find himself unable to settle here in England.'

'Not pessimistic,' she agreed. 'Realistic. There is that possibility.'

He was still looking at her, if not oddly, then certainly

intently. 'So Kirsty might end up with this place being her home, after all.'

Diane nodded, smiling. 'You've already mentioned that.'

'You have no further comment?' he prompted.

'What is there to say? I know she dislikes living in London, but she is away at school most of the time. Would you, if it did come to it, have her continue at boarding-school?'

'I'd give her the choice.'

With that, Diane agreed. 'If I were in your position, I'd do the same. I feel sure she likes being away at school, but there's still a tiny worry in case she's only putting on a brave face.'

'Agreed,' he said, seeming satisfied because she was agreeing. 'I'd probably buy a house in the country anyway. Then, if Kirsty did decide against boarding-school, she could at least be away from London for holidays.'

'Meaning you'd keep this house on?'

'For the sake of business, yes. Besides,' he grinned, 'I like it. I like London.'

'Same here. Mind you, a house in the country sounds good.' Dreamily her mind conjured up pictures of the New Forest, where she had driven miles with Nik and Kirsty in early August.

'I'd probably opt for the New Forest,' he said, frowning because Diane started laughing—frowning until she told him he might just have read her mind.

Then he was smiling, saying he'd probably buy a second home in the country anyway, irrespective of Kirsty. 'It would be nice to get away at weekends.'

Mrs Hemmingway came in with coffee, asking whether there would be anything else Mr Channing wanted.

'No, thank you.' He smiled up at her from where he sat,

his hand tightening around Diane when he felt she would change position and move away from him.

The housekeeper said her goodnights and took off for her own rooms at the top of the house, the attic floor. Except that that gave the wrong impression. Attic-like her rooms were not. Diane had been invited by her to see them, given that she and Nik had not ventured in there when he had originally shown her around the house. Mrs Hemmingway had proved to be quite friendly, detached but friendly, aware that she was no more but no less than the housekeeper, and showing no signs of being the tyrant Kirsty had made her out to be.

Even so, Diane was never quite comfortable when Mrs Hemmingway came in at moments such as this, when she was tucked under Dominik's arm, her feet curled under her on the settee. She always felt inclined to move away from him a little—and he always teased her about it, as he did now.

'I don't know why you always react like that, Diane. Anyone would think she'd caught us doing something sinful . . . I should be so lucky.'

She poked him in the ribs. 'I react like that because I'm not used to having a servant around. I never know what she's thinking about us.'

'Firstly I'm sure she's got better things to think about; secondly, let her think what she likes, if she does bother to.'

She laughed, not poking his ribs but tickling them this time, knowing how very susceptible he was to it. 'So that's the attitude I should adopt, is it?'

'Yes. And *stop that*, you wretched woman!' He moved fast, his hands whisking hers away from him. In one hand he held her slender wrists together, high in the air, and he was going to set about giving her a taste of her own treatment, until he changed his mind and kissed her instead.

Her struggle was a very half-hearted one, more a protest at the awkwardness of her position, hands bound and body twisted. 'Mmph!' It was a sound against his mouth and he let go of her. He did not free her, he let go of her hands and pulled her hard up against him, one arm tightly around her body, his other hand sliding into the silk of her hair at her crown.

There was something, just something, different about him, enough to warn her that he really meant business, and she became aware immediately of two things. She had pushed him to the point of frustration once too often and she was in what seemed to her, rightly or wrongly, a very precarious situation.

'Nik——'

'No!' His protest was stronger. With a determination which actually frightened her, his fingers laced painfully into her hair and his mouth came down on hers with a brutality she had never experienced before. This, while at the same time he manoeuvred her forcibly into the corner of the settee simply by pushing the top half of her body, effectively making her immobile.

Beneath the hungry onslaught of his mouth, breathing was difficult. A small sob forced its way up from Diane, and this was, mercifully, enough to bring Dominik to his senses—or partly so. The nature of his kiss changed, and what had been an unwelcome pressure became a tolerable one. His fingers loosened in her hair, he eased his weight from her a little . . . and then the pressure was not merely tolerable but pleasurable. Had there been any chance of her thinking of anything at all, she would have been thinking in her usual terms of danger, of calling a halt now, now, now!

Or maybe she would have thought ahead to the cross words this would inevitably lead to. But there was no chance, because Dominik was kissing her now with a sudden and exquisite tenderness, drawing from her a wonderment which seemed more physical than mental in nature. Certainly her body responded like that, with wonder, before asserting itself, quite independently, or so it seemed, and moulding itself against him in an effort to get closer, and even closer.

When his lips moved to the sensitive skin of her neck, when at last she was able to speak, all she could utter was his name. 'Nik, oh, Nik!'

But he didn't need any encouragement. His hands were already beneath her sweater, a one-time sample, loose-knit and baggy, and then his hands were on her breasts, naked as ever without a bra.

Diane's brain flashed briefly into action, but not in protest. It was, she knew, too late for that. Nor did she want to protest. The way he was caressing and kissing her now was not enough, and the time had come to stop this self-denial, this denial of him, this denial of all the love she felt for him. It clamoured as it had for many weeks to express itself in the way human love has been expressing itself since time immemorial, and she was finally going to succumb to it, to *yield* to it.

At the sudden, harsh but barely audible imprecation from Dominik, Diane's eyes came open in shock. But he wasn't looking at her, he was looking towards the door, and there, standing in the open doorway, was Kirsty.

From the look on her face the child knew, as both adults instantly appreciated, that she had walked in at precisely the wrong moment. She probably hadn't knocked on the door—why should she?

Knowing only an overwhelming gratitude that she was still fully clothed, covered, Diane closed her eyes because she had already seen enough of Dominik's attempt at composure; she had seen anger, bewilderment, disbelief and disorientation on his face all at the same time. There had also been in his eyes a fleeting . . . something resembling pain.

In a voice she barely recognised, she heard him ordering his niece back to bed at once.

'I'm sorry.' The girl's reply was tearful, frightened. 'I didn't—I couldn't sleep because I'm too excited about Daddy coming tomorrow.' And then she was gone. It was a very rapid retreat, but neither Dominik nor Diane could bring themselves to smile about that.

'You'd better go up and have a word with her,' Diane said, her voice barely above a whisper.

Nik crouched forward, dropped his head into his hands and shook it slowly. 'I can't go on like this, Diane. I've had enough of it. More than enough.'

She didn't know what to say, didn't quite know what he meant. Was he giving her an ultimatum? 'Nik, I really——'

He cut in on her, thinking she was still fretting about Kirsty. 'I'll see to her in a minute!' he said sharply, lifting his head so he could look at her. A long and ragged sigh escaped from him, a sound of utter frustration and weariness. 'Stay with me tonight,' he said, looking straight into her eyes, scanning her soul. 'Tell me now, before I go to Kirsty, that you will stay tonight, here, in my bed.'

She couldn't speak, could not answer him one way or the other. Her throat was paralysed with emotion, the threat of tears, her heart was pounding horribly hard against her ribs, terrified because this was indeed the ultimatum she could not, really, be surprised by. So, if she said no, that would be the end of her and Dominik. And if she said yes, she would find herself stealing out of his bed and into another room in the silence of the small hours.

And still she could not speak, she could do no more than look at him—but that was enough for Dominik. 'Well,' he muttered, getting to his feet, 'I think your silence has answered my question, Diane. I'll go and have words with Kirsty.' He got as far as the door before turning, adding, 'If you're not here when I come down, I'll understand.'

She wasn't there when he came down.

Nor did she sleep that night, not one wink of it. She opened her curtains to face a grey dawn and got back into bed because there was nothing else to do. She wouldn't be working today, she wouldn't be working again until after Christmas.

But the long hours of worrying, of thinking and rethinking, had been fruitless, pointless. Was it over? She didn't know. Would he ring her today? Maybe, maybe not. He would be busy with Philip, anyway, since Philip was flying in to Heathrow this morning and Nik would be there to meet him, with Kirsty.

Poor Kirsty! She had been so wide-eyed last night, eyes like saucers, frightened and guilty and not fully comprehending. She had wondered what Dominik said to the child when he went up to her. Would he have remonstrated? Tried somehow to explain? A faint smile touched her lips. Not the latter, not when it might provoke twenty questions, all of them awkward ones.

That thought, poignant as it was, brought forth the tears which had been dammed up inside her all night long. She wept, not hysterically but gently, the tears sliding down her cheeks, curling into the corners of her mouth, some trickling on to her pillow.

When the telephone rang at nine-thirty she flung herself out of bed, catapulting herself towards it because it would be, it had to be, Dominik.

It was her stepbrother, telling her that she was the only person he did not yet have a Christmas present for, and he was in an awful muddle because he just *did not know* what to get for her.

More tears came. Diane closed her eyes against them, a futile exercise, and cleared her throat noisily. 'Well, Bobby, let's see. Perhaps I can help you.' Frantically she tried to think of something which would not strain his pocket money too much, searching for ideas like a person casting for fish in a river that didn't carry any. 'Er . . .'

'Mum said you might like a scarf, but I didn't know. Do you——'

'Oh, I would like a scarf, Bobby! A pretty one, of course, one of those silky things you can wear with a nice jumper.'

'Like a decoration? Like the one you had on with that black jumper last week?'

'That's the sort, yes!' It was difficult, difficult, and she was glad when he hung up, much as she loved him.

Christmas shopping. She still had her own to finish. Determinedly she pulled herself together, took a bath, dressed and drove into the centre of Maidstone.

Dominik's gift had been bought long since; it was an expensive leather belt not unlike one he already had, one which had grown the worse for wear and needed replacing. The question was, would she be seeing him again to give it to him?

When she got back to her flat around four that afternoon, Diane's elderly next-door neighbour came to her with a big box in his hands, beautifully gift-wrapped, seasonally gift-wrapped. She looked at him blankly, because she was only on nodding terms with the man.

He chuckled at the look on her face. 'No, this isn't a gift from me, Miss West; it came for you special delivery this afternoon. Well, I say special delivery, but it wasn't a postman who brought it.'

Her heart leapt into her throat. 'Who was it?' It was a stupid question, because her neighbour wouldn't know, but if he began to describe Dominik that would be enough for her.

'A youngster, eighteen or nineteen. I had the impression he'd come from a shop or a store.'

'Oh.' She thanked the man and went inside with the box, all curiosity about its contents having faded. There was, however, a card in a small envelope attached to its wrapping and, when she read that, the curiosity returned. So did her optimism. Dominik had not signed the little card, a plain white one on which nothing was printed, but the message saying, '*Not* to be opened till Christmas Day' was unmistakably his.

Oh, the temptation to open it there and then! It was resistible only because she herself did not hold with the idea of opening presents before Christmas Day. There was that, plus the fact that she wanted to respect Dominik's wishes. So she put the box in the corner of the room, where her small Christmas tree stood, and eyed it speculatively. Then she laughed, acknowledging how good it felt to be laughing, and thought that the box was just the right size to contain a duvet. A double or a single one? Mmm. Could be either, difficult to tell. Perhaps it *was* a duvet! Maybe this was Dominik's idea of a joke? Something for her bed. A bed. Well, if it was a duvet she could count on there being another message in with it, something that would be not cryptic but teasing in nature.

Her eyes closed and she sighed loudly. When had Dominik organised this delivery, whatever it was? Not today, when he had to pick Philip up, when he would be busy getting reacquainted and handling a no doubt over-excited Kirsty and heaven knew what.

A horrid thought struck. *Had* Philip turned up? Had he actually arrived on the flight he had been expected to take?

She glanced towards the telephone and decided against it. Too obvious. Dominik was no fool, not by any stretch of the imagination.

As if mocking her, the phone rang as she was looking at it. She snatched it up and was greeted by her father. 'So you are at home? Annabel and I were wondering what you're doing tonight. Is Dominik with you, or are you expecting him?'

'No, Dad. I—this is the day Kirsty's father comes home, you've probably forgotten. But I did tell you. Anyway, he'll——'

'So you're on your own tonight?'

'Yes.' Her father and Annabel were not expecting her till tomorrow, Christmas Eve. They knew she was not seeing Dominik then, that she would not be seeing him until the party on Boxing Day evening. Not that she knew herself, now, whether she would actually be going to that party.

'Well, come round. Don't sit on your own, love, come in time for dinner.'

'No, I won't, Dad, thanks all the same. I've still got presents to wrap and a dozen other things to do, and I'd planned on being alone tonight.'

'Oh. Right then. Er——' His voice dropped to a whisper. 'You have got something for Annabel, something decent, haven't you?'

Appalled, Diane looked at the receiver in her hand. What

was her father thinking about, asking such a question? But could she blame him? No, and it was her own negligence that appalled her. She had never spoken to him about Annabel, not in private, not since they had returned from their honeymoon. She had never apologised or retracted any of the things she had said about her stepmother and her motives for marrying him. Swamped with guilt and the need to explain, to tell him she had been wrong and that her days of judging people were over, she found herself on the brink of tears again. 'Oh, Daddy, yes, of course I have. I'm—you must have seen the change in my relationship with Annabel? Surely you have?' Wrong, it was coming out all wrong.

'Well, yes——'

'What I really mean to say is, I'm sorry. I was wrong about her. Quite, quite wrong. Yes, I have a present for her, something she'll love, actually.'

It was true. Annabel loved almost all the knitwear in the range Diane was currently carrying, and had admired one sample in particular. So that was what she was getting for Christmas, not the sample but a duplicate of it, a pale pink bundle of fluff which, though bought at trade price, Diane had paid quite a lot of money for.

She hung up from the conversation with her beloved parent and wept, lamenting sorely all the things she should have said to him before today.

She did not really want to be alone tonight, she had spent far too much time on her own these past few months and had found that she did not care for it, after all. Still, it was true that she had things to do, so she set about doing them.

At nine o'clock she rang Dominik because she couldn't stand it any longer, hoping against hope that it would be he and not Mrs Hemmingway who answered.

A strange voice answered, a male one. Philip Nolan, presumably. She hesitated, stammered and plunged in. 'I—i—is that Kirsty's father, Mr Nolan?'

'This is Philip Nolan, yes. Who is this, please?'

'I'm—my name is Diane West. I'm a——'

'Diane! Oh, sorry about that! It's just that I feel I already know you, I've heard so much about you from Kirsty and Dominik. But it isn't me you want to talk to, is it?' he went on, before she could comment. There was a smile in his voice and he sounded like a pleasant man, very pleasant. 'I'm afraid Nik isn't in, though. He's just discovered he's run out of Scotch and he's gone in search of some. Mrs Hemmingway will *not* be pleased to learn about this,' he added, *sotto voce*, 'because Nik's supplies of booze are her responsibility and she clearly didn't put Scotch on her shopping list. She's lurking in the kitchen right now, and when she comes in with the coffee-pot she's bound to ask where the dear boy's gone.'

Diane didn't try to resist her laughter. The inappropriate description of a *lurking* Mrs Hemmingway, who was anything but a lurker, was highly laughable. And, not only that, Philip's reference to Dominik as 'the dear boy' was also amusing. 'Then tell her,' she managed, 'that Nik's gone to buy a box of those cigars he smokes now and then.'

'Oh, I couldn't do that!'

Was that indignation in his voice? 'Why not? You could spare her feelings, Philip.'

'No, no, she'd still be chagrined.'

'Let me guess, she's supposed to keep him supplied with cigars, too. Right?'

'Right! The dear boy's spoiled rotten, don't you know?'

'No comment. Anyway, it was nice to talk to you and that was my reason for ringing, actually. I just wanted to be sure that you had arrived—safely.' She added the last word hastily, wondering whether he had any idea of the speculation he had been responsible for.

'Well, I have.' Another smile in his voice. 'Thank you for caring—and I look forward to meeting you at the party. Or am I likely to see you before Boxing Day?'

'No, no, you're not, Philip. Goodnight, then.'

'Goodnight.'

It was quite satisfactory, really. She had made her move; Philip would tell Nik she had phoned, and why, and if Nik felt he needed an excuse to ring her, he had one now.

He did not ring, not until eight-thirty the following morning. Diane was sound asleep and she was not thrilled at being woken by the telephone. She picked it up, and she snapped instantly awake. 'Dominik?'

'I just said it's Dominik.' He was irritable, not at all the man she was used to. Fortunately, he made it clear that his displeasure was not aimed at her, not at the moment, not this time. 'Philip told me you rang last night.'

'Yes.' What else should she say? She was wondering about the dryness in his tone.

'Yes. At ten minutes past twelve. Just as we were saying goodnight to one another. *Then* he decided to remember, *then* he decided to tell me.'

Diane bit back a smile. 'Well, he was probably tired from his journey and everything.'

'Not him.' That was all he said, and Diane scrabbled around for something else to say, forgetting completely the box which had been delivered—until her eyes alighted on it in the corner.

'I—thank you for the Christmas present.'

'You haven't opened it?'

'Certainly not! I never open pressies before the day,

Christmas, birthdays or whatever.'

'Good girl.' A pause. 'Well, I shall look forward to seeing you with it on Boxing Day.'

'What?'

'Boxing Day. The party. Philip's honour. We—I, mainly—have dredged up a number of his friends from the past, some of whom were able to make it to the party. Of course, several of them are musicians of one sort or another so—heaven knows what we can expect. I don't doubt that their numbers will double, for one thing.'

Diane was hardly taking this in. All she was concerned about was the fact that he was still expecting her. Expecting her to be at the party. Letting him know none of her doubts, she said, 'What time do you want me?'

Another pause. Low laughter. 'There's really no answer to that, my darling.'

'I meant——'

'I know what you meant, you idiot. Eight o'clock—eight o'clock sharp, in your case. Earlier if you like and can manage it. In fact, the earlier the better,' he went on, his voice softening. 'Diane?'

'Yes?'

'I . . . nothing, really. I just like talking to you. Have a happy Christmas, darling.'

'Happy Christmas, Dominik.'

She remained standing by the phone when he'd hung up, feeling tearful again. So it hadn't been an ultimatum! She flopped into a chair, still tearful but happy, too, feeling as though she had spent the last twenty-four hours in an emotional mincing machine.

Her eyes caught sight of the box again, curiosity arising almost irresistibly. Almost. She went over and picked it up, sensitive to the weight of it now. Well, it could be a duvet, but it wasn't a duvet. Nik had given her a clue, sort of, when he'd said he looked forward to seeing her with 'it' at the party. So, unless he was expecting her to wear a duvet, or to bring one with her for reasons which must remain unfathomable . . .

The following morning, first thing, she tore off the Christmas wrapping on the mysterious box, legitimately because this was Christmas Day.

'Happy Christmas, Darling. Dominik.'

There was another card inside, and that was what it said. It was between the outer wrapping and the box itself, which was white with gold lettering on it. Her eyes widened as she registered the lettering. It had come from a well-known furrier's in Bond Street and it was *not* a duvet!

It was a mink coat.

CHAPTER TEN

GINGERLY, almost reverently, Diane lifted the full-length garment from its box and stared at it.

A mink coat?

Instantaneous thoughts and pictures, wildly diverse, crowded into her mind in a jumble. She could not accept this! She absolutely could not accept a mink coat from Dominik! What would her father think? And Annabel? She giggled, getting carried away, thinking they might jump to the conclusion that it was Nik and not she who was paying the mortgage on this flat, that she had become a—what was the expression?—a kept woman! A rich man's mistress!

What idiocy. As if they didn't know her better than that.

There was no way she could keep it, lovely, *gorgeous* though it was.

He had known exactly, precisely what would please her. But of course he had, for the mental picture in her mind now was a memory. Several weeks ago she had shown Dominik her range of simulated furs, because he had expressed an interest in seeing all her samples, the leatherwear and the knitwear, too. And when she had come to one particular fur she had slipped it on, modelled it for him. The memory was vivid in her mind, her standing in the middle of her spare bedroom, empty except for a garment rail, and the remarks she had made about the fur, her favourite of the range because it was just her in style with its classic simplicity. Collar and revers, four buttons at the front—two plus two, double-breasted—concealed pockets at the hips, a half belt at the back, length a fashionable just-below-the-knee.

'This,' she had said to him, 'I adore! Except that it's simulated,' she had added laughingly. 'I mean, they've got the colour right. The manufacturers call it "Ranch". But it isn't the real thing. It would be much nicer in mink, wouldn't it?'

'I suppose it would. Or sable?' He had smiled at her questioningly and she had gone on, encouraged by his interest in her samples.

'No. Well, not for me. Mink would be my choice.'

And that had been the end of that. Except that it hadn't.

She stood, foolishly, thinking she must ring him and tell him there was no way she could accept a gift like this, not really registering how she was holding it against her cheek, loving the feel of it against her skin. But before she phoned she would just try it on . . .

Perfect! It could have been made especially for her. When she picked up the phone to ring its donor, she had the coat on—though it didn't look too good with an ankle-length nightie.

'Dominik?'

'None other. Happy Christmas.'

'Dominik, I—yes, happy Christmas, darling.'

At the other end of the line, Dominik closed his eyes. Darling! Never, ever had she called him that before. Not her. Not his hot and cold, catch me if you can, I'll always keep you guessing *mystery* woman. 'What? What do you mean, you can't keep the coat?'

'I mean I can't. I just can't. The neighbours would gossip.'

'For heaven's—you're *not* serious?'

She hooted with laughter. 'No. Not about the

neighbours. But I am about the lavish, extravagant Christmas present.'

'But it was made especially for you!'

'It was?'

'Of course it was. From a sketch done from memory.'

'By whom?'

'By me, you twerp. I have talents you have not yet discovered.'

Diane was momentarily silent at her end. To *that* there was no answer!

'Are you still there, Diane?'

'I'm still here. How did you know my size? Or is that a stupid question?'

'Very stupid. Size twelve. And even if you hadn't once told me that yourself, I'd have known. In any case,' he went on, trying and failing to suppress the smile in his voice, 'while I'm not as familiar with your body as I intend to be, I do have a certain——'

'Enough said, Dominik.' She tried to sound stern but she failed pathetically, she was too distracted by his 'I intend to be' rather than 'I would like to be'. 'Well, look,' she continued, 'I've no wish to offend you but I really——'

'Can, *will* keep the coat. Wear it tomorrow night,' he said, and hung up, effectively telling her that his gift was not to be talked about any further.

Diane wore the coat. She had been through a battle royal in her own mind—yet she had known all along she would lose it. Or win it. Quite simply, she wanted to keep the coat.

A faint powdering of snow was scattered over Knightsbridge when she rang Dominik's doorbell the following night. Kirsty was by his side, glowing and excited when Nik answered the door. And it was she who spoke first, rambling on about the extension on her bedtime tonight, about her father and his looking forward to meeting Diane, about how she had told him all about her grown-up friend who was her best except for Lizzy MacIntyre at school. She did not notice how Diane's eyes had fixed on those of her uncle, fixed and held. And how they were smiling as much as his were smiling.

It was as if Kirsty wasn't there. Dominik opened his arms and Diane walked in to them, hugging him and feeling no self-consciousness when he kissed her fully on the mouth in front of his niece.

'Hmph! At it again.' Kirsty looked bored, if not vaguely disgusted. 'Daddy's upstairs and he's waiting to meet you. You're the first to arrive, you know.'

Of course she was. It was only six fifty-five.

Philip Nolan, a drink in his hand, got to his feet with a look of respect, immediately followed by a slight narrowing of his eyes when Diane walked into the living-room. He was taller than she but a fraction short of Dominik's height, thin but good-looking, with a mop of longish hair which was the exact blond of his daughter's. And his eyes were identical to Kirsty's, or rather hers were identical to his, as blue as blue could be. A light but very positive blue, alive and sparkling, interested, curious . . . appreciative of what they were seeing.

He turned at once to Dominik, placing a hand on his shoulder. 'Dark horse, Dominik. You always were. Why didn't you mention that Diane is gorgeous?'

Dominik didn't answer; his only response was to look at Diane in such a way that she could not interpret what he wished to convey. Was it a warning look? A 'listen to him, this is typical of him' look? *What?*

There was no time to find out. There was no time for

much of an exchange, either, because the doorbell rang and in that very same instant Mrs Hemmingway put her head around the living-room door, asking whether she should go down.

'No, I'll get it,' Nik said. It was just as well he did, and it could so easily have happened differently—he could so easily have said yes to his housekeeper. But he didn't, and that was fortunate because this particular party was doomed with gate-crashers not at the eleventh hour but before it had even got started.

Dominik reappeared two minutes later, looking thunderous. 'Philip, I opened the door to some friends of friends of friends, drunk as skunks and insisting they'd be welcome here.'

Philip was the picture of innocence and, to be fair, Diane believed he was. 'Don't look at me, Nik. I'm not even sure who's going to turn up legitimately tonight.'

Nik took the point. He contented himself with, 'You're an oddball, Philip. Always were.'

'What does that mean?' Kirsty wanted to know.

Her father put his glass down, swept her into his arms and lifted her high in the air. 'It's just another way of saying I'm eccentric, sweetheart.'

'Oh. Well, I do know what eccentric means.'

'You do?'

'Weird. I think you might be a bit weird, Daddy.'

'And is that a bad thing?'

'Noooo! I like it. It means you're not boring.'

Diane watched father and daughter with interest; she watched very closely to see how genuine Philip Nolan was—and she was satisfied that he loved his daughter very much, despite what could have been deemed as evidence to the contrary. He had been tied to a contract, and that had to be borne in mind.

By the time ten-thirty rolled around, Kirsty had been in bed, if not sleeping, for half an hour. Half an hour during which Diane had been collared—no, cornered—by her father, who was still very sober but talking about his daughter non-stop. He was, she realised, feeling very insecure and uncertain of the future and of his ability to handle his eleven-year-old daughter. Even though she would be away at school for the most part, he still seemed to view her as something of an unknown, much as he loved her.

In the corner of the room, behind the piano, someone was playing a saxophone and playing it beautifully. It was a young man who, although not exactly inebriated, looked as if he were somewhere between this world and the next, out of it, in love if not exactly making love to his instrument. At the piano was an old and, as Diane was reassured, very dear friend of Philip's, someone he had not seen for three years, since their paths had last crossed when they'd met with much surprise and much pleasure in a nightclub in Capri.

Then Dominik was there, suddenly, angrily interrupting Philip's conversation with Diane to tell him baldly how he was feeling. 'For heaven's sake, Philip, I've got my doubts about you. I mean, I have really got my doubts about you!'

'What—dear boy, what *are* you talking about?'

Dominik glanced quickly at Diane before answering. 'I won't repeat the offer I've just had from that—female over there. I'll leave that to your own imagination, but I will say this: if these are the kind of people you normally mix with, then I am going to worry and worry in earnest about the influence you and your cohorts are going to have on my niece.'

There was a stunned silence. Beyond it, the saxophonist and the pianist played on.

'Nik——' This, from Philip, looking aghast and worried. 'I'm afraid I—you're not being fair!'

Diane intervened; it did not occur to her that she shouldn't. 'Take it easy, Dominik. This isn't Philip's fault, the party wasn't his idea. You thought you were making a nice gesture, I know, by looking up old friends for him.' She turned to Philip, anxious to keep the peace between the two men. 'He went to a lot of trouble, you know, to make this a good party for you.'

'For goodness' sake! I know that, Diane, and don't think for one moment that I don't appreciate it. Look, Nik, bear with me, let me find myself again. Here in England, I mean. I'm—it's all—just give me a chance, man!'

He looked at Nik, as did Diane, and Nik cooled off visibly. 'All right, all right. I'm just not used to this kind of scene. Half of these people are as high as kites, they were when they arrived, and make no mistake, Philip,' he went on, getting angry again, 'if I see the first sign of evidence I shall throw them out bodily. Do you understand me?'

'Perfectly, dear boy.'

Diane was subjected to a glare then. Why, she had no idea. Dominik vanished in the direction of the kitchen and she turned to Philip, feeling embarrassed.

'What,' he asked, 'is your relationship with Dominik, exactly?'

It was a good question. She paused, shrugged, hesitated. 'We're friends.'

'Friends?' His eyebrows rose. 'Just friends?'

'Yes, Philip.'

'Let met get you a refill,' he said, taking the glass from her hand. 'It was just tonic, wasn't it?'

'I'm afraid so, I have to drive home tonight.'

He smiled. 'But of course. You and Dominik are just

friends.'

When he came back to her he said, sighing in a way that increased her sympathy towards him, 'I'm in need of a friend myself, Diane.' He glanced around him, making her realise fully that which she already knew. These people were not his friends; they had been once upon a time but they were only acquaintances now.

'I know,' she said gently, because he really was a nice man and Dominik was still thinking in terms of the Philip Nolan he had once known. But that Philip had gone and, soon enough, Dominik would realise that. He had made a nice gesture in organising this party, but—it wasn't working. Philip had spent very little time talking with the people here, except for Diane.

'Well,' she went on, reaching impulsively to touch his hand, 'I hope we can be friends, Philip.'

He looked at her quickly, uncertainly. 'I hope so, too. Oh, I do hope so. I—look, may I ring you some time? I mean, Kirsty will have your number, won't she? It's—you know her better than I do, you know who and what she is today, I mean——'

Diane's heart went out to him; he was struggling and she did know what he meant. 'Of course you can ring me. Any time.'

They talked on, they talked almost exclusively alone amid the vaguely bizarre atmosphere around them—until her eyelids were drooping and she simply had to call it a day.

When she got to her feet, Dominik was there, appearing as if from nowhere, as if he had been watching but unwilling to approach her before. Her. Or Philip.

'I'll see you to your car.'

He did, and her car was just a hundred yards further along the street. 'Nik, I have to say this, you're still not giving Philip a chance. He's not, he does not *feel* right with all those people, not any more. He might have at one time but—oh, you know what I mean. Bear with him and——'

'I'm trying, I'm trying very hard to, believe me.' He looked angrily down at her. 'But as for *you*——'

So he was angry with her. Why? She never got the chance to ask him because, as if it were designed deliberately to aggravate him further, the sound of the saxophone made itself heard, a sudden but plaintive explosion piercing the silence of the street.

'Enough.' Dominik's voice was dangerously quiet. 'Enough is enough is enough.'

'Dominik——'

He shook her hand from his arm. 'They're out, all of them. If I don't throw them out we're going to have the police around here sooner or later—and that I can live without.'

Diane didn't know what to do, what to say. She had never, ever seen him this angry before. 'Please, Nik, calm down! Just ask them to go, I'm sure they will. Do it peaceably, please!'

He made an effort to get hold of himself, she saw him doing it and she loved him for it. Loved him, loved him, loved him. 'I'll try. I'll try it that way first, at least.' He turned back to her, dragging his attention from the sounds emanating from the first floor of his house. 'All right, Diane, go home, and take care driving. You didn't drink too much, did you?'

'Do I ever when I'm driving?'

'OK.' He nodded, still seeming displeased. 'I'll talk to you tomorrow.'

But he did not talk to her the next day. It was Philip Nolan who rang her, in the morning, thankfully not too early.

'Diane?' His anxiety made itself felt down the telephone line. 'It's Philip. I—could I talk to you? I mean, can we meet? I would suggest lunch, but Kirsty and Nik—will you have dinner with me tonight? Can you do that? Late-ish because I can't very well leave Kirsty and Dominik——'

'Fully understood.' Diane was perfectly calm, hoping it would communicate itself to him because, if he did but know it, he really had nothing to worry about. 'Yes, I'll meet you for dinner, Philip. I have nothing arranged with Nik for tonight. Tell me where and when—or would you prefer me to suggest?'

'Please do.'

She kept it simple. 'Oxford Circus, the exit from the tube on the north Regent Street side. Nine o'clock? Good. We'll meander and find somewhere where we can eat and talk.'

He began, effusively, to thank her, but she stopped him because it really was not necessary. 'I think I can take it that you and Nik have had a row?'

'Something like that.'

'Nine o'clock,' she said firmly. 'I'll be on time, Philip.'

And she was. And she was satisfied, by the time she parted from Philip at eleven-fifteen, that her own action in meeting him for dinner was fully vindicated and that it was not Philip but Dominik who was behaving like the 'oddball' now.

She was sure that was the case. But, when Dominik turned up at her flat at precisely eight fifty-two the following morning, any doubt she might have had would have been swept away forever. If she had thought him angry the night before last—well, she just didn't recognise him now.

Still half asleep, she stood like a piece of furniture inside her own front door, unaware of what was to come, of what, in the form of Dominik, would confront her when he stepped out of the lift.

'What the bloody hell are you *thinking* about?' He roared the words, his greeting to her, so loudly that she stepped back inside her flat involuntarily, both frightened and flabbergasted.

'Nik! What on earth is the matter with you? How can you—how dare you?' Anger rose to meet anger like an old acquaintance who, while not caring for its mirror, rises up none the less in recognition.

He stood, superior in height and glaring at her, kicking the front door shut with the heel of his foot. 'I was informed this morning on surfacing that the *appointment* my brother-in-law had last night was with *you!*'

'So?'

'So? *So?* So I want to know where, when, how, why, and most especially, *what!*'

'And what the hell is that supposed to mean?' That she looked far from being a spitfire in her ultra-feminine nightdress and négligé, Annabel's Christmas gift to her, never crossed Diane's mind. Nothing spliced into this moment, her rage, her fury. Nik's fury. 'Dominik, *what* are you implying?'

'I'm implying nothing,' he roared. 'I'm *telling* you I hate this, it stinks. I'm telling you that Philip monopolised you entirely at the ludicrous party I gave for him and I'm telling you that he could not take his eyes off you! I'm also telling you that *you* did nothing to discourage his attention.'

Diane's mouth fell open, literally fell open and, for the life of her, no words could emerge from it because speech was a million miles away. She could only stare at him dumbly, riveted as she was by this gap, this chasm, these aeons of difference between what she knew and what Dominik thought he knew. With a stiffness that was nothing less than glacial, she told him to go. 'Get away from me! I will not be spoken to like this, and I will not entertain your ridiculous suspicions a moment longer. Go. Get out of here. How *dare* you?'

For one awful, sickening instant she thought he was going to strike her. He went white and he went rigid, standing as stiffly as she was, glowering at her as if she were an object of fascination, a short-lived fascination which was both riveting and disgusting at the same time, to be dismissed as unworthy of further time in studying.

He turned, he went, he opened the door and he slammed it so hard that it seemed not only her flat but the entire building shook on its foundations.

Stunned into immobility, Diane stared after him, stared at the closed door fixedly like one who had heard word of the four-minute warning which meant the end of everything, everything in existence, sooner or later.

And *that* was not real, it couldn't be. It couldn't happen, ever, because the world was not that mad, and neither was she. Neither was Dominik. Her hand shot out for the door-handle. She had to call him back, *now*! Before it was too late!

Dominik was half-way down the corridor, heading for the lift, before he stopped in his tracks, before sanity, at least in some semblance, returned to him. But, when it did, it did so in a torrent of realisation so massive that for seconds he could do nothing but stand immobile, as if he were a figure in a tableau. It started as a trickle, the sanity, and then the dam which had been inside him for weeks, for many, many weeks, for longer than he had realised, burst and out the realisation came flooding.

He wanted her. So what the devil was he doing, walking away from her? He loved her. He loved her as he had never dreamed he could love anyone, ever!

His hand was raised, poised in mid-air, ready to batter on her door, when suddenly it opened and she was there, crying like one demented, and he was holding her, crooning to her, holding her and touching her, revelling in her.

Diane tried and failed to get a hold on herself, it was more than she could do. 'You must let me explain,' she cried, dangerously close to tears. 'Philip and I, it was as innocent as——'

'It's all right, you don't need to explain.'

'No! I want to, it's important. Please, Nik! When he rang to ask me to meet him, he told me that you and he had had a row. We spent two hours together in a restaurant and I just let him tell me his troubles, that's all. He said there was no way you would listen to him because——'

'Because I was jealous.'

'No!' It was not with exasperation, but with sheer frustration that Diane shook her head. 'No, he hadn't realised how he'd aggravated you in that respect by monopolising me at the party.'

When Nik looked at her blankly, she almost laughed. 'Oh, darling, you really haven't taken it *all* into account, have you? Philip . . . he felt embarrassed the other night.'

'Embarrassed? By what?'

'By several things. He felt embarrassed and awkward because he found he had nothing to say to his old friends, not any more. And you were angry with their goings-on and Philip didn't know what to do. He explained all this to me over dinner. That was one of the reasons he stuck by me at the party—he was trying to show you——'

'One of the reasons?' Dominik interrupted, as if he were

not quite convinced.

'Sticking with me was Philip's way of showing you he had nothing in common with the others. Don't you see?'

'Yes,' he said, but it was a dubious sound. 'Though it would have saved us a lot of misunderstanding if he'd just *told* me how he felt.'

'But that was another reason he felt embarrassed, Nik. He felt awkward because you'd gone to the trouble of having the party for him, but it was all going wrong!'

This was met with a shrug. 'That didn't matter.'

'It mattered to Philip.' Relieved, Diane went on quickly to explain Philip's motives and behaviour further. 'He also wanted to talk about Kirsty. He had no idea he was annoying you by cornering me, he simply needed to talk about Kirsty, which was the other reason he stayed by my side. Do try to understand, Nik: the prospect of settling in England again feels strange to him, and what with Kirsty . . . well, let's just say he needs some support in the confidence stakes.'

'Which I haven't given to him?' It was more of a statement than a question and, knowing she had made him understand, Diane put her arms around him. 'Not yet, but you will.'

'What makes you so sure?' he asked, half smiling now.

She looked up at him, her own smile radiant and full. 'Come on, I know you very well, Nik, and I can assure you of two things: Philip has no interest in me as a woman, nor I in him as a man. He saw me only as a go-between—between you and him. You see, he cares what you think, and he loves and cares about his daughter even more than I'd realised.'

'And what makes you say that?' Nik wanted to know, looking both relieved and hopeful.

'Several things, but I'll just mention two of them. Firstly,

Philip is going through mental gymnastics in regard to the location of the house he's going to buy. He knows Kirsty hates London, but that's where most of his work is going to be in future, so he's hoping to compromise and find something on the outskirts, so that both the country and the city are in easy reach. Secondly, he must have asked me fifty questions about Kirsty's current thinking, about where she's at, if you see what I mean. Now just ask yourself—is this a father who doesn't care? It this a man who isn't going to do his utmost to look after his daughter and make her happy?'

'No.' Nik was really smiling now. 'It sounds as if he really has reformed, and I know for a fact that Kirsty wants to be with him. Perhaps—well, maybe I should be more patient with him.'

Diane smiled inwardly this time, knowing she need say no more on the subject of Philip. She had helped to make the peace between him and Dominik, and she knew Dominik would keep to his word about being more patient.

She was looking at Nik still, looking and briefly reliving, suddenly, those long and awful moments when he had slammed the door behind him earlier, when she had thought he had gone from her life for ever. About to say something, something jocular over the fact that they were still standing in the hallway, she suddenly found herself being swept off her feet. Held high in Dominik's arms, she was carried, oh, so willingly, into her living-room—where she was placed gently on to her feet, swaying slightly.

'Marry me,' he was saying. 'Marry me, Diane, and swear you will never, ever spend another day in which you won't touch me and love me as I love you. Oh, darling! I love you so much, I just can't begin to describe how I feel.'

In the face of her stunned silence he rushed on, seemingly

convinced she was still angry with him. 'Diane? Why are you looking at me like that? I didn't really think you were interested in Philip, honestly I didn't, but I did feel jealous and angry with the way he——'

'Sssh!' Gently, laughingly, she put a finger to his lips, but he brushed her hand away, urging an answer from her.

'Say it, Diane! Say you'll marry me just as fast as we can arrange it. Let's go away to the sun together in January as man and wife.'

And then she was crying, crying, of all things! Oh, foolish tears. How could this be, when all she wanted to do was to tell him that she loved him, too, that she loved him to distraction, that she had loved him for a long time? 'Oh, Nik! Nik, just listen to me. I've waited and waited and wanted and yearned to hear this, I've wanted for a long time to tell you how much I love you.'

But now, at last, she could begin to.

HARLEQUIN
Romance®

Coming Next Month

#3049 ANOTHER TIME, ANOTHER LOVE Anne Beaumont
Laurel Curtis isn't planning to change her status as a single mother. A
traumatic experience with one man was enough. Connor Dyson, an Australian
property tycoon buying the lease on her flat, has other ideas—like taking over
Laurel, too!

#3050 PARTNERS IN PASSION Rosemary Carter
Teri comes back to her grandfather's African game farm where eight years
ago, before she had to move with her parents, she had loved Rafe—and
thought he loved her, too. Now Rafe greets her as a stranger.

#3051 FACE VALUE Rosemary Hammond
Christine agrees to do one last modeling job before she changes careers. John
Falconer, however, has devised the assignment of a commercial for his
company simply to meet her—and he offers Chris another proposition entirely.

#3052 HOME FOR LOVE Ellen James
When interior designer Kate Melrose is hired to redecorate an unknown
client's home, she falls instantly in love—with the house! But she soon falls
even harder for its owner, the handsome, irascible Steven Reid.

#3053 THE CHAIN OF DESTINY Betty Neels
When Guy Bowers-Bentinck comes to her rescue, Suzannah, alone in the
world and without a job, is forced to accept his help. Not that she wants to be
beholden to such an infuriatingly arrogant man!

#3054 RASH CONTRACT Angela Wells
Karis doesn't welcome the reappearance of Nik Christianides in her life—
reawakening tragic memories she's spent years trying to suppress. Now,
though, she has to listen to him because he has a way of replacing what she
had lost.

Available in May wherever paperback books are sold, or through
Harlequin Reader Service:

In the U.S.
901 Fuhrmann Blvd.
P.O. Box 1397
Buffalo, N.Y. 14240-1397

In Canada
P.O. Box 603
Fort Erie, Ontario
L2A 5X3

**In April, Harlequin brings you the
world's most popular romance author**

JANET DAILEY

No Quarter Asked

Out of print since 1974!

After the tragic death of her father, Stacy's world is shattered. She
needs to get away by herself to sort things out. She leaves behind
her boyfriend, Carter Price, who wants to marry her. However, as
soon as she arrives at her rented cabin in Texas, Cord Harris, owner
of a large ranch, seems determined to get her to leave. When Stacy
has a fall and is injured, Cord reluctantly takes her to his own ranch.
Unknown to Stacy, Carter's father has written to Cord and asked
him to keep an eye on Stacy and try to convince her to return home.
After a few weeks there, in spite of Cord's hateful treatment that
involves her working as a ranch hand and the return of Lydia, his ex-
fiancée, by the time Carter comes to escort her back, Stacy knows
that she is in love with Cord and doesn't want to go.

**Watch for *Fiesta San Antonio* in July and
For Bitter or Worse in September.**

JDA-1

You'll flip . . . your pages won't!
Read paperbacks *hands-free* with

Book Mate · I

The perfect "mate" for all your romance paperbacks

Traveling • Vacationing • At Work • In Bed • Studying • Cooking • Eating

Perfect size for all standard paperbacks, this wonderful invention makes reading a pure pleasure! Ingenious design holds paperback books OPEN and FLAT so even wind can't ruffle pages — leaves your hands free to do other things. Reinforced, wipe-clean vinyl-covered holder flexes to let you turn pages without undoing the strap . . . supports paperbacks so well, they have the strength of hardcovers!

Pages turn WITHOUT opening the strap

SEE-THROUGH STRAP

Reinforced back stays flat

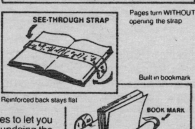

Built in bookmark

BOOK MARK

BACK COVER HOLDING STRIP

10 x 7¼ opened
Snaps closed for easy carrying, too

Available now. Send your name, address, and zip code, along with a check or money order for just $5.95 + 75¢ for postage & handling (for a total of $6.70) payable to Reader Service to:

Reader Service
Bookmate Offer
901 Fuhrmann Blvd.
P.O. Box 1396
Buffalo, N.Y. 14269-1396

Offer not available in Canada
*New York and Iowa residents add appropriate sales tax.

BM-G